DOUBLE BLIND

DOUBLE BLIND

A Novel

Michael J. Vaughn

iUniverse, Inc.
New York Lincoln Shanghai

Double Blind

Copyright © 2006 by Michael J. Vaughn

All rights reserved. No part of this book may be used or reproduced by any means, graphic, electronic, or mechanical, including photocopying, recording, taping or by any information storage retrieval system without the written permission of the publisher except in the case of brief quotations embodied in critical articles and reviews.

iUniverse books may be ordered through booksellers or by contacting:

iUniverse
2021 Pine Lake Road, Suite 100
Lincoln, NE 68512
www.iuniverse.com
1-800-Authors (1-800-288-4677)

This is a work of fiction. All of the characters, names, incidents, organizations and dialogue in this novel are either the products of the author's imagination or are used fictitiously.

ISBN-13: 978-0-595-41807-7 (pbk)
ISBN-13: 978-0-595-86151-4 (ebk)
ISBN-10: 0-595-41807-4 (pbk)
ISBN-10: 0-595-86151-2 (ebk)

Printed in the United States of America

For Katrina Galway

She had had boyfriends, had made love, but Rodin's work she knew to be something else, something about power and surrender and weakness and force and then all those things getting mixed up, so that you couldn't tell which was which. They weren't actually two figures. They were some kind of storm. Some kind of storm at sea with the clouds and waves and winds tossed about, and was it the sea that made the rain or the rain that made the sea?

—JCWatson, from *Current Wisdom*

CHAPTER 1

My mother wanted me to be a doctor. But I knew how awful I was with people, so I botched the exam. She expressed her disappointment for years.

Mom was a cabernet alcoholic, much more elusive than your square-bottom whiskey swillers, your pitcher-a-night barflies. She carried on for years, hidden by her custom wine cellar, her weekends in Napa—and never, ever tired of complaining about her wretched, alimony-fueled existence.

One day in Calistoga, she jumped the embankment, her brain swollen from all-day tastings, and planted her Jaguar in the crown of a live oak. Watch the picture in stop-motion, drunkie Mom rocketing through the windshield, dangling seat belt erect with inertia, a jag of glass slicing her head clean off.

I was relieved. Relieved to get on with my life without the constant board review, the endless filibuster, the eternal making up for my father's desertion (when I couldn't really blame him). I was also relieved that she hadn't taken anyone with her. I always thought she would.

I'm a drunk, too. Half the time that shit touches my lips, I end up behind bars—or married. There's your free will, your predestiny. The fault lies not in our stars, but our *cells*.

It's 1973. A psychiatrist, Donald Goodwin, rounds up a pool of 67 Danish children—sons of alcoholics, adopted soon after birth by non-alcoholic parents. Didn't matter. Eighteen percent became alcoholics, compared to five percent of the control group (sons of non-alcoholics, adopted by non-alcoholics). Dancing to the tune of their DNA, they were three to six times more likely to become alcoholics.

The tune I dance to is science. I love the human body. I love every part of the human body except the larynx, which produces so much more shit than the colon. Abolish the larynx, give me mutes for patients, and Voila! I'm a doctor.

I haven't had a drink since the bachelor party. Whenever I drive past a liquor store, I picture 23-year-old Davey, climbing a live oak in his paramedic jumpsuit to fetch my mother's noggin from the high limbs.

It's four o'clock Tuesday. I run the last of my gels, give the high sign to Marty Quock (my guardian, my wing-man) and hop on my bike for a ride down Palm Drive. Palms are not a native species here, but they give the campus a regal entranceway, leading through small twin towers to El Camino Real, highway of the Spanish missionaries. (We call it "The El Camino," which translates as "The The Road.")

I track the spooky sidewalk underpass, tunneling under the train station, then reemerge in the townie chaos of Palo Alto. Cars stack up at the light as pedestrians scatter across like pigeons. I wing a right at the bead shop, lock my bike to an S-shaped rack, and cut around to the side door. My secret knock (the opening beat to "My Sharona") is answered by the sexiest woman on the peninsula.

Kelly's got one of those short, mousse-dependent haircuts that spindles out like an old broom, falling from her crown in triangles of black and purple. For her it works, because she's got the face: long lines, sharp chin, Mediterranean nose with a midway bump, brown cat's eyes and a loose-lipped smile. She's the library book I always check out.

"Hey, Hoppy. In for the usual?"

"Sure. How about you?"

Kelly turns around, bends over and flips her skirt. She's painted her ass like a hooker's face: blue eyes with overlong lashes, a broad nose straddling her crack, and pouty lipsticked mouth surrounding her bubble-gum labia. She has pre-lubed herself with massage oil, so my mission is clear. I open my fly, give my dick a couple of pulls and ram it home. Then I close the door.

"Oh!" she groans. "God! I never feel complete without that cock in me. Could you just follow me around the rest of the day?"

"I think the necklace-makers of Palo Alto would frown on it."

"Charge them admission!"

I slide out till nothing's inside but the helmet, then thrust back in. The blue eyes jiggle.

I was waiting for a train to San Francisco, taking the kids to a Giants game. Laura tapped her finger against a bulletin board.

"Daddy! Look! It's a cat with a tuxedo."

Or a picture of a cat, name of Corialanus, on a "Lost" flyer. I spotted the same cat ten feet away, on a "Found" flyer, tore them both down and said, "Look, Laura—two of a kind!"

She screwed up her face. "Does that beat…a straight?"

"No. But it will give us a happy pet-owner."

"You don't know what it's like!" said Kelly. "I've got a seven-year-old who's been mooning over that cat all week."

"I could hazard a guess," I said.

"Let me buy you dinner."

"I have this 'wife' thing. And you sound entirely too good-looking."

She laughed. "I am. But how can you tell?"

"I'm a geneticist."

"Of course! How 'bout coffee?"

I thought about it. "Coffee's safe. Four o'clock? University Café?"

"See you there. I'll be wearing denim."

Indeed she was. And a necklace of lapis lazuli. I might have been okay if it weren't for that necklace—kept drawing my eyes to her cleavage. Milk-white. I'm a sucker for goth girls. But I was *not* the one who brought up sex.

"The single-mom thing is hell," she said, chewing a biscotti. "The men all think I'm looking for Daddy number two, when all I really want is a robust fucking. I think that's why I'm so attached to the goddamn cat. Hah! I must have walked right by that 'Found' poster."

A half-hour later, she was perched on the break-room table at her bead shop, legs splayed as I pounded into her. I certainly don't mind foreplay, but there was something thrilling about a woman who treated you like a human dipstick. Afterwards, I conducted some negotiations.

"I don't love my wife. I never have. But she's the one who's raising my kids. I have a vested interest in keeping her happy. How about once a week? We get off, we don't get too attached—you get to keep your prospects open."

I reached for my wallet and extracted two hundred-dollar bills.

"Before your mind goes anywhere near convention, let me say that this a free-will offering, an acknowledgement that some people get the shaft and others get rich wives. But there are attachments. Don't tell me about your boyfriends, don't tell your boyfriends about me. Use a condom with your boyfriends. Are we agreed?"

4   Double Blind

Kelly smiled and folded up the bills. "You're a real good fuck, Hopkins. But I will take your money."

This time is different. She stops me, takes me out, and I finish in her mouth.
"We're hungry today?"
She peers around my dick sort of…shyly (what kind of a trick is that?).
"I like it, once in a while. You taste pretty good. Nutty-fishy. A touch of almond."
"I'm on a tasty-sperm diet," I say. "What some men won't do to please their…"
"Looking for a noun?"
"Why does 'lover' sound so fucking French?"
"Don't worry," she says. "I doubt you'll ever have to introduce me at a dinner party."
I head for the bathroom to clean what's left of Kelly's ass-hooker from my privates. When I come out, she goes in, and I take the opportunity to fetch my wallet. Kelly's been pretty good, but I still like to maintain a certain mythos about the process—as if the money appears by magic. I open my usual drop-spot—a brass box engraved with Hindu figures—and find it occupied by a hunk of yellow glass, cloudy like lemon marmalade, size of a horse-pill.
"What's this?" I ask.
She re-enters in her bathrobe. "Trade bead from Kenya. Made in Venice, fifteenth century. I thought you'd like it."
"I do." I drop it in her pocket. "Keep it here for me."
She frowns. "Shithead."
I tap my temple. "Smart shithead." Then I slip on my windbreaker. "Next Tuesday? Lover?"
She hesitates. She has every right to say no. I wouldn't blame her. "Yeah. Next Tuesday."
"See you then."
"Shithead."
There's no time I like better than Tuesday evening, wheeling past the immigrant palms of Stanford. Relieved of my lust.

CHAPTER 2

The kid is twelve, going on huge. Six foot, a hundred and eighty pounds. One time, a high school football coach was jogging by, and stopped to inquire.

"That goalie out there. He's one of the coaches, right?"

"That's my son," I said. "A twelve-year-old gargantua."

"Wow! Any interest in football?"

"Not a whit."

"Do me a favor, wouldja? Take him to a 'Niners game."

"Will do."

I watched him jog off, certain that I would never see him again. Marcus has size, and coordination, but he's too damn nice to play football. He hates the idea of ruining someone else's fun. By, for instance, taking the ball away. He runs his goalie box like an isolationist country, willing to patrol his borders but not to take proactive action in adjacent regions.

He certainly doesn't get this from his parents. Jessie and I are two of the most aggressive, selfish assholes I know. I've even tried to pass on some dirty tricks from my high school days.

"Y'see, Marc, when you're the goalie, you're protected. The ref has to keep the other players from messing with you. There was this one game where this pesky little striker was buzzing me every time I came out for an easy pickup. It was pissing me off, so the next time I stayed low till he made his little run at me, then stood up real fast and clipped him in the shoulder. Hah! Little bugger spun three times and fell on his ass. Then the ref called a foul on *him*! Because I had the ball, and it was his obligation to stay out of my way."

Marcus gave me a puzzled look. "But that doesn't seem very…nice."

6   Double Blind

"Nice?! Son, *he* broke the rules, and I was *nice* enough to illustrate the error of his ways."

He just looked at me. I love that kid like nobody's business, but I wish I knew what species of extra-terrestrial impregnated my wife.

When I get to the park, it's that cool, murky twilight, when the kids are all tired but still looking for that perfect Beckham boot to the top right corner. Pietro the wonderkid is lifting lazy crosses from the right sideline; Marcus stands patiently in the goalface, waiting till one of his teammates gets a head or a foot on it. Some of them go in. He doesn't care. To step out and intercept one of Pietro's lovely arcs, to deny the midget forwards their due glory, would be unpassably rude.

What kills me is that Marcus rarely lets in more than three goals a game. If he had even the least bit of aggressiveness, I would be answering calls from Team USA. But now he's jogging my way, so I jam those thoughts into my back pocket.

"Dude!"

"Hi Dad."

I give him a hearty hug and pound him on the back. Hard to believe this big ol' piece of horseflesh is my son.

"Ouch! Dad!" he whines. It's not the pain, but the embarrassment.

"How was practice?"

"Same ol', same ol'."

I don't know where he picks up these old-fashioned expressions. I swear, one time he said "Hell's bells."

"Dad, what's that gunk on your sleeve?"

"Well for God's sake," I say, thinking quickly. "It's that viscuous thortazine we've been using at work."

He laughs. "Better be careful. It looks like lipstick."

He has pierced me, like a butterfly on a collection board. But you can't explain to a twelve-year-old the sad compromises of life—how you pay a single mom to fuck you so you can keep your family together.

"All right, joker." I grab the back of his neck and steer him toward the car. "You and me got a date with a pizza parlor."

"Glory be!" he exults.

The reviews on the pizza are mixed. Laura greets us with huzzahs.

"All right! Did you get pepper-shlomoni?"

"Would I get a pizza without pepper-shlomoni?" I flip open the box to reveal a sea of oily red circles.

"Pepper-shlomoni!"

"And a vegetarian pizza for Mom."

My wife appears in the hallway, holding a bell pepper and a paring knife. She also has the pissed-off stare, the one that never seems to leave.

"What am I supposed to do with the dinner I'm halfway through preparing?"

Ten seconds in the door and already, a minefield.

"I left a message on your voicemail."

"I've told you before, that doesn't work!" Her voice is working up to school-marm nasal. "Laura's been on the computer, so the line's been tied up. Is it too much to ask that you speak with me directly before you go making executive decisions?"

And here we are, back in our familiar tracks. Jessie loves fighting, because fighting is the only way she knows if I still care about her. I guess if I didn't, I wouldn't fight back.

I throw up my arms. "Executive decision? It's a goddamn pizza!"

She's in my face, drilling me with those beady blue eyes. "What have I told you about swearing in front of the children?" But I have a stopper.

"What children?"

Jessie looks around at an empty living room. I can hear the bedroom doors closing, the music coming on. It's a familiar strategy—I used to do the same when Mom came home drunk. My debate points come at a cost, however. Jessie heads for the kitchen at full rant, gesticulating like an Italian chimpanzee. Because I'm an idiot, I follow.

"I try so hard to maintain some kind of normalcy around here, and you constantly undercut me. Is this why I gave up my life, to look like an idiot in front of my own children?"

I set down the pizzas, searching the memory banks for some way to quell this, to buy a little peace for my poor, scared children. But Jessie's still ranting, and chopping vegetables, which is not a good combination.

"A little respect, Hopkins. A little goddamn consideration. We're supposed to be a partnership, a united front. You think it's easy, running this household with you out there…fucking around? Nailing some perky-titted coed who stops by the lab to give you blow jobs?"

She's been making this accusation since our first anniversary. For ten years, it wasn't true. But at least, for a moment, she has fallen silent. I recall a time when I could calm her down with a touch on the shoulder—and I make my move. But Jessie is a loaded spring, and when she feels my hand she spins around to swat me away.

At first, I don't feel a thing. Then, a curious warmth beneath my left eye. I touch it with a finger. I see red. And then I don't see anything.

A year after my master's, I was still in Berkeley, working as a lab assistant. I got a strange call from Gunnar, my old lab partner, and met him in a coffeehouse. He looked nervous, like an actor before his first entrance.

"You know I like skiing, right? I go skiing…a lot."

"Sure, Gunnar."

"This last weekend, I am at Squaw Valley, and I am on the tram, going to the top. When the tram goes past the first tower, it swings forward, you know? And I hear a woman, she says, 'Woo!' And the woman, she is Nancy."

"My Nancy?"

"She has the white jester's hat? And the lime green suit?"

"Y-yes."

"And she is…with a man, and they are getting very…fresh. And I am thinking, I cannot tell this to Hopkins but for I am very sure. It is late, the last run of the day, so I follow them down—a long, long way. At the bottom, they turn in at a cottage, and…they go inside, together. And so I am thinking still, I must have more…" He rolls out his hand, trying to finish the sentence.

"Evidence?"

"Yes. So. I ski to the back, and I find a window, and I peek in." His face flushed, and he was having a hard time looking at me. "Hopkins? Please…ask me to go on?"

My insides felt like a sand castle at high tide. But going back was not an option. I took a long breath.

"Gunnar, please…tell me."

He stared at the tabletop. "She was kneeling, and had the man's penis…"

"Stop, Gunnar. Please."

For me, going on a rampage has a small price of admission: one drink. After that, I was out every night, roaring drunk, on the make. I fucked sorority sluts, desperate fifty-year-old barflies. A housewife in her van, outside a laundromat. A fat chick with big tits in a broom closet at the library. A beautiful black woman gave me a blowjob in the alley next to a nightclub. I stuck my dick in half the holes in Northern California. And then I got venereal warts.

One Saturday morning, I rubbed lotion into my poor penis as I ruffled through three weeks of mail. At the bottom of the pile was an offer from Stanford: a five-year study, "gene expression patterns of breast carcinomas." A month later, I was standing at a kickoff party in Palo Alto when a good-looking woman came over and started asking questions. She wore a leather miniskirt, tight-fitting sweater, eyeshadow like an Amazon warrior. I guess I was easy pickings. The female gender had simply worn me out.

I don't remember much else. I didn't have to. Jessie made all the decisions. She was nuts about me, she was 35, and she wanted children. She was the path of least resistance. She was also fierce, and skinny, with a sharp hawk's face and a tiny butt.

Gentlemen. The do-gooders and bullshit artists will tell you to ignore that quaking in your balls, those baser instincts that make you respond to certain women and not to others. Do not listen to these people. If you do, you might wake up someday, two children later, and discover that one of your eyes is missing.

"Mr. Grinder! Good to see you moving. Here, let me give you a little help."

A bee stings my right arm; the pain in my face subsides. My right eye registers a bank of blinking lights on large, blocky machines. Toward the window, an old woman lies next to her respirator, staring at the ceiling.

"Where…?"

"Stanford Medical." She's a short, dark-haired woman with broad lips and round, black-brown eyes. Her features are so expressive they're almost cartoonish. *It must be hard*, I think. *Going around with your feelings right there on your face.*

"I'm Dr. Pisarro," she says. "You can also call me Lisa. You're a lucky boy, Mr. Grinder. A half-inch higher, we'd be in some serious trouble. We've put in ten stitches, and given you a patch to keep your eye from moving around. Your wife is outside, so let us know if you'd like her to come in for a visit." She folds her fingers and gives me a serious look. "Also, I need to know if you'd like to talk to the police."

I do find myself considering it. But hazardous gesticulation is not a crime, and my children's lives have been disturbed quite enough.

"No," I reply. "My wife is terribly clumsy, and a little spastic. And yes, do send her in, please."

Dr. Pisarro gives me a long study, scouring my face for hints of deception, then gets up and walks away. She is wearing black polyester pants that show off her ass, the kind of bubbly, compact butt that short women often have. I am grateful.

Jessie comes in with red eyes, her face worn to the pink with crying. One look at my patch and she starts all over, gripping my arm as she declares her sins.

"Oh God Hopkins I'm so sorry I had no idea I forgot I had it in my hand oh *shit* I am so sorry!"

She ducks her head to my shoulder and weeps luxuriously. I wrestle my arm free and cradle the back of her head. This episode means that I will have to make love to my wife sometime this week, so I will have to conduct a visual harvest. Sliding in and out of that uninspiring pussy, holding her legs together for friction, I will need to conjure some other woman's body to bring me over the top. Someone I barely know. Someone highly inappropriate.

Fortunately, Lisa Pisarro has returned for her clipboard, and is now walking away. I pull my wife closer, so I can get a better look.

CHAPTER 3

❀

The patch has taken away my depth perception, adding a technical challenge to an already tricky situation. Kelly is dangling ass-up from a trapeze-style sex swing as I receive her pink slot on my prick like a schoolboy catching apples on a knife. On my seventh foray I misjudge, and jar my member on her left cheek.

"Ouch! Damn."

Kelly's smile appears somewhere near her left knee.

"Dontcha mean 'Ahrrr!'?"

"Oh!" I complain. "Poking fun at the disabled."

She lets out a girly titter. "Seems more like the *disabled* is poking *me*. But you really do look like a pirate, Hoppy. Maybe we should go out and buy some costumes."

"Whatever you want, hon. But for now, could you give me a little massage?"

She tumbles forward into a handstand and flips to her feet.

"Damn, woman!"

"Used to be a cheerleader." She rubs a handful of oil between her palms, then applies it my injured penis.

"Ah, thank you."

"Can I see it?" she asks. I lift up the patch to reveal my stitches.

"Aigh! That bitch. How could she do that?"

"Don't you think I kinda deserved it?"

"Hoppy. A kick in the ass, maybe. Laxatives in the coffee, okay. But no one should go for the eyes."

"She didn't do it on purpose."

"Or so you think."

"Yeah, okay. She's definitely getting…edgy. I worry about my kids."

12   Double Blind

She stops the rubdown. "I worry about mine." Then she eyes my penis, which has regained its vigor.

"Lie down, honey. Let me do the work."

Quite a cowgirl, my Kelly. She knows all the angles, when to work the tip, when to grind it in, when to treat me like a carnival ride. I'm gone in five minutes. She frigs herself off as I shrink inside, then tumbles next to me, fingering her nose ring like a genie with a wish.

"I've got an idea."

I arrive at the soccer match in a bitter, distracted mood, not exactly the ideal sporting parent. The team makes matters worse by playing in a sloppy, uninspired fashion. Even Pietro is off; he blows three chances in a row by lofting the ball over the bar.

"Pietro!" I shout. "Keep it low! Make the keeper play it!"

I have broken one of my own rules: don't coach unless you're the coach. Our actual coach, the Norwegian import Nils Arntsen, gives me a look that's hard to read.

Just before the half, our sweeper, Jackie Marchetti, catches a cleat and stumbles, leaving their middle striker a clean path to the goal. Marcus follows the textbook, charging forward to cut down the striker's angle. But then he stops, five feet away, and is back to his usual reactive stance. The striker—who is not center forward for nothing—taps the ball to his left, swings his foot around and boots it in. Marcus is disappointed, but not enough. When halftime arrives, I meet him halfway to the bench.

"Marcus, where are your eyes in relation to mine?"

He looks at me, taking a measurement.

"Same...level?"

"Yes. And do you know what that means?"

He ducks his head, like a dog who thinks he's in trouble. I cup a hand on his shoulder.

"Son, it means that you're a really big kid. And everyone out here knows that. Do you realize that you could have thrown yourself at that kid's feet and taken the ball away? He wouldn't have done a damn thing."

Marcus scrunches up his face. "But Dad, that doesn't seem very..."

"Fair, Marcus? Was it fair that your defense left you stranded? Was it fair that that striker can shoot with either foot? It's not fair or unfair, it's just using what you've got. Life will throw shit at you every day, and I want you to learn…to take advantage of your strengths. Listen, I don't ask too much of you, right?"

"Sure."

"You know how we make you try all the food on your plate? Well, now, I'm asking you to try this. The next time you get hung out like that, I want you to leap at that ball and steal it away. But I'm warning you, it's just like lima beans. You might end up liking it."

He smiles, and I feel better. The kid's so damn nice, I worry about pushing him. He jogs to the bench and grabs a quartered orange. As the second half starts, I drift down the sideline toward Nils.

"Sorry, Coach. Don't mean to be a buttinski. But I used to be a keeper."

"Oh!" says Nils, flashing that great big-toothed grin. "Usually it is only the parents who know nothing who butt in."

Marcus's second half is largely uneventful. Pietro has regained his form and is controlling the game, setting up beautiful give-and-gos with his wingers. He receives one of these at the top of the penalty box, punches it to his right and—as if he has actually paid attention to me—hits a screamer across the grass. The ball touches down in front of the goalie and skips crazily, rocketing under his arms and into the net.

That one ties it up, but then the defenses clamp down, turning the game into a neutral back-and-forth in the middle third of the field. With five minutes remaining, their winger makes a dash down the left sideline and sends a low cross to the top of the goalie box. The right striker makes a nice leaping header, but Marcus is ready, diving full-out to swat it away.

He doesn't swat it far, however; it settles ten feet away, to the right of the goalface. The two nearest players, Marcus and the right striker, are horizontal, but not for long. Marcus claws forward with all four appendages, looking all the world like a charging bull. The striker springs to his feet, takes two steps and slides forward, hoping to jab the ball toward the goal.

They meet in a pile. The ref blows his whistle. The striker gets up, holding his knee. Marcus stays down. Nils grabs his first-aid kit, and we're off. I pick my way through a ring of players to find Marcus in the fetal position, his body curved protectively around the ball. He grips it in both hands, eyes closed in pain. Nils is pounding a chemical ice pack into activation. Marcus's right shoulder is not where it should be. I kneel and touch his arm.

"Marcus. You can let go of the ball now. They called time-out."

Marcus opens his eyes, squinting against the sunlight.

"I got the ball?"

14 Double Blind

I laugh. "You damn well did, son."

"Oh God, Dad. It hurts!" Marcus is balancing his weirdly sloping shoulder on the passenger-side door, trying to keep it from moving.

"Son, remember how I asked you to try something new today? I want you to try something else. I want you to swear. Swearing is good for pain."

"I don't know, Dad. Mom says…"

A car cuts into our lane and I hit the brakes, jamming Marcus's arm against the door.

"Fuck! Shit! Hell's…bells!"

"Jesus, Marcus. You been watching cable?"

Marcus manages a sheepish smile. "Pietro gets all the movie channels. Hey, Dad? I think my shoulder slipped back in. Sick!"

"Good, Marcus. I think that's good."

"But it still fuckin' hurts."

"Son, let's not get carried away."

He snickers, as we pull up to the emergency room.

A young Japanese nurse comes to take X-rays, then slips out to process them. They return in the hands of Lisa Pisarro. She spots my pirate patch and smiles.

"Well! The Grinder family is having a week."

"Yes," I say. "But this one came in a moment of glory."

She eyes Marcus's cleats. "Did you win the battle?"

Marcus grins. "Yes."

Pisarro clips the X-rays into the reading light.

"You're lucky it went back in. Otherwise, I would've had to pop it in myself, and I'm already banned in three states due to certain…excesses of my ultimate fighting career."

Marcus is such a gullible kid, he doesn't quite catch the joke. Pisarro signals the jest with those big eyes of hers and manages to get a chuckle out of him.

"However," she continues," we still have some issues. You see, when your shoulder separates like that, it stretches out your tendons. We're going to give you a sling that holds your shoulder up to the collarbone, so your tendons can tighten back up. Should take about three weeks. After that, however, you still need to take it easy, because these things have a tendency to repeat. I'll send Keiko back to rig you up. Meanwhile, Jolly Roger, try to keep the rest of the family from maiming itself, okay?"

"Will do," I reply, and give her my best schoolboy smile. Pisarro leaves us in a half-dark room. Minutes creep by, and no Keiko.

"Hey Dad."

"Yeah?"

Marcus smiles. "I did kinda like it. Taking the ball away."

"Good." First Pietro, now this. I should quit genetics and go into coaching.

"Dad?"

"Yeah?"

Marcus chews on a thought, gazing at the image of his warped shoulder on the far wall.

"Is Mom gonna be all right?"

"What do you mean?"

"Wuhl, like, when she cut your eye last week? I sorta…wasn't surprised. I mean, like, sometimes I'll ask her something? Something easy, like, What's for lunch? Or, Can I go to John's house? And she gets all spastic, like, waving her arms around and stuff. And then she starts talking about wasting her life, and she just can't handle it, and why don't you ask your father. I can't even talk to her, Dad. And sometimes, I really want to."

My huge kid, the one who's borne a separated shoulder without crying—he looks terribly small.

"You're not gonna leave, are you, Dad? Pietro's dad left, and he never came back."

I place a hand on his good shoulder and look him in the eye.

"I'm never leaving, Marcus. I won't ever do that. Your mom and I are going to get some help. You just hang in there, and be real nice to her, okay?"

He sniffles and nods. I bend over to kiss the top of his sandy blond mop.

Keiko arrives to fit Marcus with his sling, then hands him a couple of analgesics and a cup of water. We exit the ER to find the entire soccer team gathered in the parking lot, weaving passes between SUVs and Beamers. When they spot Marcus, they break into that raucous tribal barking that I thought had gone out of style.

"Did we win?" says Marcus.

"Nah," says Pietro. "But we tied. We put Wehner in goal. He was pathetic."

His teammates laugh and poke Wehner in the ribs. He swats them away like gnats.

"But he did make a pretty good save," Pietro allows.

"Hey, Marcus," I say. "Why don't you guys stay here and make fun of Wehner some more..." I pause for laughter (twelve-year-olds are my best audience). "And I'll go get the car."

"Okay," says Marcus. As I leave, he's giving gory details of his injury; his teammates respond with obscurely hip adjectives. I walk along the ER windows, lined with miserable faces, and wave to Nils, who's standing at the front desk (and probably looking for me).

I sit in the car, and gaze at the green lights of my cell phone, hooked up to the cigarette lighter.

Does anybody use these things to light cigarettes anymore?

It's a phony thought. I'm stalling, because I need to give my wife a full report. It's getting dark, and she is certain to be gathering anxiety like valence electrons. This will undoubtedly be my fault. Never mind that boys get injured in soccer games every day. Never mind that I have granted my son his first moment of fearlessness. My place of residence will continue to be hell. Because I have gone and made my son a promise. I take a deep breath and press the buttons.

"Kelly. It's Hopkins. Let's do it."

CHAPTER 4

Prairie voles are extremely monogamous creatures. They rarely take second mates—even when the original mate dies (picture those couples who jog in matching outfits). The secret of this attachment is endorphins.

When prairie voles mate, the female produces an endorphin called oxytocin. If you inject a female prairie vole with oxytocin, she will bond with a male just by being in his presence—something that would normally occur only after intercourse. If she is injected with an oxytocin antagonist, then has intercourse with a male, she will fail to bond with her partner. Leaving a very confused and hurt male vole.

Damon is a remarkably clean-cut individual. I'm huddled with Kelly in a biker bar in Redwood City—hoping to avoid anyone who might know Jessie. Damon enters in a slash of sunlight, wearing a baby blue golf shirt, khaki shorts and blazing white tennis shoes. His hairline lies in that midpoint between receding and bald, giving him an open, friendly appearance, an effect that's further assisted by a broad shotgun smile. He's that neighbor who's constantly inviting you to barbecues, and not minding when you don't show up.

Kelly greets him with a hug, then turns him my way like an action figure.

"Hopkins, this is Damon."

I shake his hand. I have no idea what to say, but Damon needs little encouragement.

"Kelly's told me all about you! And I am truly sorry about your predicament."

I take a swig of Coke and study the room, putting on the appearance of a customer who's willing to say no.

"What I'm trying to understand, Damon, is…what exactly do you get out of this?"

Damon smiles, eager to tell his story.

"First of all, I'm a trust fund baby. So money is not an issue. I'm also a child of divorce. My little ventures often enable parents to stay together till their children are grown. So I like that. Thirdly, the women are tremendously grateful. Most of them have gone without passion for years, and they let off the kind of sparks you just don't see in the happily married types."

He can't contain that sparkling grin. He's getting to the good part.

"Now I confess my baser nature. I am a connoisseur of the hunt. Any idiot with a full head of hair and chiseled pecs can klutz into a lay now and then, but a guy like me has to work the angles. Especially when I have to forgo the advantages of natural chemistry and go after an assigned target. I won't chase just anyone, of course, which is why I ask for photographs. You should see some of the scary-looking…Well, rather not be negative. On the positive side, your Jessie is just my type.

"But let's be clear. Even though I find her attractive, I do not blame you in the least for not feeling the same. I consider marriage a wholly unnatural state. What we all desire is newness. I acknowledge that need in myself, and I think I've developed a pretty unique way of dealing with it. But I always seek permission from the husband, because my other desire is to not to get myself killed."

I take a long drink to let this all settle in. It's a peculiar situation, but to any male willing to cop to his true nature, Damon's thinking is reasonable. I look at Kelly, who's watching me like a gambler at a spinning slot machine.

"Nothing abusive?" I ask.

"Out of the question."

"Safe?"

"Condoms at all times."

"What if we end up in divorce court?"

"I don't know you from Adam. There's no deal here, no money changing hands."

My small five percent of doubt is washed away by the picture of my son, crying in the ER.

"Damon, you have your assignment."

Damon fires that grin.

"Hot damn!"

It's Thursday, two days after the unofficial deal. Mood-wise, I'm a little under the weather. My reference batch didn't include any RNA from the lung—in genetics terms, a must-have—and I had to toss three works' worth of tumor arrays. Sometimes I feel like the only capable person in a world of morons. I'm trying to keep this toxin self-contained, but I'm pretty sure that Laura has picked up on it. Instead of giving me the standard Interesting Things That Happened to Me in Swim Class, she's tapping her index finger against the knuckles of her left hand.

When we pull into the driveway, my wife is standing under the magnolia tree, holding one of its milk-paddle blossoms to her face. She spies one-half of her family, squints her eyes with pleasure, and forms an expression with her mouth that resembles a smile.

Laura's no dummy, she runs to the parent who's in the better mood. Jessie grabs her around the waist, lifts her skyward and pockets her neatly against her hip.

"Hi," I say. "Sorry we're late."

"Oh," she says. "Are you late? I've been out here, gardening. Beef stroganoff tonight?"

"Mmm yeah." I plant a kiss on her cheek. She looks at me, and I can read her thought: *First that nice man at Draeger's, now my husband. I've got it goin' on!*

Draeger's is an upscale grocery store in Menlo Park—and my insider's tip for Damon Karvitz. Each Thursday, Jessie drops Laura at the pool, does her shopping, then heads for the upstairs café (latte, non-fat, two shakes of semi-sweet chocolate). I picture Damon at the railing, scoping the luscious house-wives at the checkout stand. He spots his target, sliding up the escalator. After that, it's a ruthlessly simple plan: condiment table, ask for the time, a strategic nutmeg spill. He puts on just enough charm to make her hope to see him again, to make her glow just a little—to inspire her to cook her husband's favorite dish.

It'll take a while. I have given Damon a worthy challenge: a woman con-vinced by years of neglect that she is wholly unattractive. Which brings me to my dilemma. Now that m'lady's endorphins have been activated, do I have sex with her? Would it hinder Damon's campaign, by lessening her justification for cheating, or encourage her, by convincing her that she does, indeed, have it "goin' on"?

I check on our kiddies asleep in their chambers (Marcus's shoulder afloat on a concatenation of pillows), then report to the bedroom, where my wife is gazing at herself in the mirror.

"What are you looking at?" she says, good-naturedly.

"Same thing you are," I reply. "Did you have a good day?"

She smiles, Mona Lisa.

"I guess I did."

I come from behind, reach a hand around her waist, feel the swell of her breast.

I always get the kids when they're well exercised.

This is my thought as Laura plods along the sidewalk, pool-wet hair, rubbery limbs. She falls into the passenger seat and straps herself in.

"Hi, Dadsalish."

"Hi, Lauralish."

We were watching some swishy British comedy when we latched onto the "lish" thing. Now it's a ritual.

"How was swimming, babe-alish?"

"Just delish." She waves her hand downward like a Jazz Age socialite.

"Delish?! You're not drinking the pool water, are you?"

She clucks her tongue. "Don't be ridicalish. It *feels* delish. Capish?"

"Capish." I rev the engine and head for home. My mind, however, is fixed on espionage.

"Laura?"

She gives me a stern look. I correct myself.

"Lauralish?"

"Yeh-ess?"

"How's your mom? Is she doin' okay?"

This knocks her out of her "lish" mode into something more serious.

"She seems…happy."

"And what do you mean by the big…pause?"

"Wuhl. She's happy, but she's not always…there. Like last night, she asked me if I wanted some ice cream…"

"And you said yes?"

"Well, duh!" she says, answering my straight line. "But Marcus and I were watching a movie, and I kinda forgot. But when the movie was over, I went to the kitchen, and my ice cream was sitting on the counter, with whipped cream and fudge, and it was all melted into goo!"

"Which you ate."

"Well, duh!" She giggles, then returns to the serious face. "Are all moms like this?"

"Sometimes. But I think she'll be all right. We're…working on a few things. Just hang in there, okay?"

She stretches and yawns dramatically.

"Okay, Dadsalish."

I'm traversing the archways of Stanford's quad, picturing my wife having sex with Damon Karvitz. Neither one of them is what you would call bodyphotogenic, but they're having fun, and that's what's important.

I'm heading for a Saturday lecture that I don't need to see. My real objective is to open up Jessie's schedule for freelance nookie. When I told her about it, she promptly set up the kids for an afternoon with the grandparents and headed off on some "errands."

Thankfully, the onset of adultery means that my wife no longer feels the need to have sex with me. Kelly's vision of my contented cuckold's life has come true. I am the happy geneticist, widening the scope of his knowledge in a public forum. I enter a packed lecture hall (God bless Palo Alto) and settle for the rightmost seat in the front row. It's a rainy September day; a breeze noodles under the windowsill to tickle the back of my neck.

Our lecturer, Arthur Poulterbryce, is in the wrong business; he ought to be a stand-up comic. He pulls up a graph on the overhead and says, "You'll see in this comparison that the group suffering from depression gives a much more negative response to the same question. Of course! They're depressed!"

People don't expect brain researchers to be funny, so the laughter carries an extra density. A dark-haired woman, front and center, is laughing so hard she's losing her breath. Dr. Poulterbryce gives her a look of mock disapproval—which makes her laugh even harder. The woman is Lisa Pisarro.

After the lecture, I pick my way through the crowd, and catch her in front of Memorial Church.

"Mr. Grinder! You're stitchless."

I run a finger along the tiny buttons of skin over my cheekbone. "Took 'em out myself. Used to be a pre-med student."

"It looks good. How's your son?"

"Indomitable. He goes out to the driveway every night to shoot left-handed baskets. So where are you headed?"

"The Gates of Hell."

Aren't we all? I think. Then I remember it's a bronze in the Rodin sculpture garden.

"Why don't you come along?" she says. "I could…use a chat."

There's something inside that pause, but I'm just along for the ride. We cross the courtyard and turn for the art museum.

"That Poulterbryce sure had you in stitches."

She giggles at the thought. "Oh! I know. Arthur and I are friends from way back. He's a little too deft at pushing my buttons."

"Did you enjoy it? I mean, the lecture?"

"Most of it I know already. Arthur keeps me well briefed. But it's nice to see all those laypeople, lined up at the trough of knowledge."

We stop before the Shades, a trio of muscular bronze men, oppressed by some great weight. Rodin bent their necks at painful angles, forcing the tops of their heads into a tabletop line.

Pisarro blinks at a sudden sunbreak. "You've heard of Camille Claudel?"

"Rodin's lover," I reply. "Model, muse. Though I'm a bit fuzzy on the…"

"She spent her last thirty years in an asylum," Pisarro fills in. "They said she could have been as great as Rodin himself, but she suffered from what today we'd call depression. She destroyed everything she made, with one exception: a bust of her…brother."

Pisarro melts before my eyes, shoulders slumped, legs wavering. She stumbles forward and buries her face in my jacket. I take the cups of her shoulders in my hands, and am overcome by a rush of fragmentary thoughts: the raven thickness of Pisarro's hair, the exaggerated fingers of the Shades—the way that someone's tears, in a cartoon, can flood a whole town.

She catches her breath, lifts her face from my lapel, and speaks without looking up.

"I'm…awfully sorry. My brother tried to kill himself yesterday."

"Don't worry," I say. "You heal my wounds, I'll…"

"It won't heal." She spins away, her hands shaking. I feel small in her presence.

"Please go," she says. "I'm sorry. I shouldn't have…"

Her thought trails off. I stand there for a moment, then turn and walk away.

CHAPTER 5

Being Jessie's husband is not always bad. I am seated in the second row at the Paul Masson Winery in Saratoga as Chris Isaak floats a high note. I am close enough to see my reflection in his boots.

The seats belong to Richard and Darlene Zwei, Jessie's parents—as does the VIP membership that allows us to spend intermission inside the old chateau. Richard brings a couple martinis to the balcony, where the Silicon Valley spreads out before us like a streetlight wheatfield. I study the ice crystals on the surface of my drink, then lob Richard a sports prelude.

"Bonds."

He chuckles. "Most ungodly hitter I ever saw. Did you see that ball he hit the other day?"

I shake my head, concurring with his disbelief—the high arc, the landing in the Bay, the scrum of orange kayaks going for the grail.

"Is he gonna catch Aaron?"

Richard sips, shuffles the juniper across his tongue. "Entirely up to him. Fire in the belly. That clock is ticking, though. One serious injury…"

None of this is important. The object is simply to exchange words. We observe the ten-second pause between subjects. The air around us is a hive of sounds: a hundred bursts of laughter, two hundred footsteps, the slam of thirteen doors. Richard rubs a hand over his silvered mustache.

"Jessie seems downright…bubbly. Has she picked up some new medication?"

I laugh appropriately. "It's like living in a rainy environment," I say. "Lots of clouds, lots of the time, but when the sun does come out, it's brilliant."

"You have a flair for lowered expectations. Not that I'm criticizing. The women in this family are lunatics. Keep a close eye on Laura. Ah, there's *my* nutcase now, calling me in to charm the pants off of one of her friends. Stay here a little longer—enjoy the peace. I'll cover for you."

"Thanks, Dad."

Richard walks away with that Deep South amble—a limp from Vietnam—and I am left alone with gin, vermouth and the lights of the South Bay.

I love that man. In a world composed mostly of shit, he is the closest thing I've found to actual grace. Unlike my own father, he didn't let a crazy wife drive him away. I hope I get him in the divorce settlement.

I chew my olives and rejoin my wife, who takes my hand as we head back to our seats. A drift of fog settles over the ridge like a phantom crop of Chardonnay. Chris opens the second act with "Baby Did a Bad Thing."

I am flat on my back on the eighth green of the Stanford golf course. The maple tree above me hatches a trio of leaves, which descend like paratroopers and land right next to me. Kelly sputters awake.

"Pfft! Jesus!"

"Wait a minute. You're naked on a public golf course and you fall asleep? How does one go about doing that?"

She laughs and reaches for my dick, which has begun to shrivel in the night air.

"One gets oneself roto-rooted by a manly man."

I grab her moon-white butt and heft her across me like a blanket, then I notice the surface of the green.

"Damn! Divots."

She giggles and slides upward till our genitals are rubbing. I don't anticipate a second erection, but here in the open—cars whooshing by on the expressway—it sure feels nasty.

"Tell me something, Miss Kell. I know you're not necessarily getting reports from Damon, but I'm having a hard time understanding the effect my wife is having on men."

This seems to catch her interest. She stops her gyrations and cocks a pierced eyebrow. "You want to give me some examples?"

"Sure. We took Marcus to watch his team in the playoffs. Jessie walked over to say hi to Nils, the coach. Nils reacted like a thirteen-year-old asking a girl to the dance. I mean, he squirmed! Then there's our mailman, Peter. We're on the usual small-talk terms: How ya doin', nice weather. But yesterday, Jessie comes out on the porch and surprises him. He hands her the mail and speeds off like he's seen a ghost. A couple hours later, a carful of boys drives by while she's out gardening and shouts 'Hot Mama!' Like they've rehearsed it."

Kelly snickers into her hand. "A drive-by flirting!" She taps a finger against her nose, giving my stories a thorough analysis. "So what's your wife's reaction to all of this?"

"She's so blissed out it's hard to tell, but I think she's enjoying it."

"Sort of a power trip?"

"Yeah."

"I think that's your answer. Power. Boys in a car, they'll yell at anything that moves. But the men…Your wife's pretty intimidating to begin with. Damon has added a certain sexual charge, and the combination is probably a little overwhelming."

I spot a quarter moon cutting up through the trees and consider her conclusion. "Yeah. I could see that. Should we start back?"

"Yeah. I think we'd better."

Our luxurious weekend is the payout from several synchronicities. My blessed in-laws made off with the kids for a trip to Mammoth Lakes. Jessie made up some story about an ill friend in Placerville—where she is, no doubt, being plowed silly by Damon. And Kelly just happened to be house-sitting at a country estate across from the golf course.

We're traversing San Francisquito Creek when I spot a light coming from the pool house.

"What's that doing on?"

"Kevin's down there with his friend Arvind."

That freezes me. "Kevin? Son Kevin?"

"Yes. Son Kevin."

"Goddammit, Kelly!" I whisper-shout. "I told you…"

"I know what you told me," she says, full-voice. "Did it occur to you that this could be a tremendously fun experience for my child?"

"Yeah. And if you had told me he'd be here, I wouldn't have come. I am not comfortable with your kid getting any impression of me as a father figure."

"Oh you're so fucking gracious! Like you're doing Kevin some goddamn favor. Everything you do is for the sake of one person—Hopkins Grinder—and nobody's kid, yours or mine, figures into the eq…"

I grab her by the arm.

"I do everything for my kids, and you have no fucking right to say otherwise!"

26   Double Blind

She shakes my grip and rubs her arm. If she had a paring knife, my eyes would be in jeopardy.

"What about fucking me?" she says. "Are you doing that for your kids?"

"As a matter of fact—yes."

"Asshole!" she hisses, then turns for the house. I can hear her muttering curses all the way up the path. I turn to see Kevin and his friend watching me from the pool house.

I consider the jacket that I've left in the house and decide that it's dispensable. I get out my keys, and head for the car.

Two days later, I'm the last one in the office, finishing a grant report. I'm almost done when I hear the steady pad of athletic shoes—Marty Quock, coming down the hallway.

Marty's the senior scientist, and therefore the guy I come into the most contact with. He's a finely balanced blend of mellow but professional, with a quirk or two to make things interesting. With his gangly frame and round spectacles, he's got the bookworm vibe nailed, but he's also into nude beaches and those impossibly perfect Japanese anime girls.

He peers over the top of my cubicle like an anxious prairie vole.

"Marty! What's up?"

"Hi, Hopkins. Are we...alone here?"

"Far as I know."

He nudges his spectacles, trying to balance them on his thin nose. "It's very important. I need to tell you something, and it's very...sensitive information."

I stand and lean against my desk to give Marty my full attention. He rubs an earlobe between thumb and forefinger, the most favored of his nervous gestures.

"I do not wish you to think badly of me, Hopkins. By telling you about this...item that I have found, I reveal something about myself that is not so flattering. But I feel I must do so, regardless."

He's certainly got my attention. And now he's rubbing the other earlobe.

"What is it, Marty?"

He reaches for his wallet and extracts a Post-It note, folded in half, temporarily sealed.

"Please, Hopkins—wait till I'm gone. And when you pull it up, make sure that no one can see. I'm...I'm very sorry."

He walks away quickly, down the hall and out of the office. I open the Post-It to find an Internet address. I take a survey of the grounds, then angle my monitor toward the inside of my cubicle.

When I punch in the address, the screen fills up with blue squares, then the squares turn into pictures. The first is my wife's mouth, wrapped around Damon Karvitz's penis. Damon is one well-hung motherfucker.

A heading appears in gaudy orange—*Horny Housewives*—followed by a block of text: *Watch our studly trio as they chase down married hotties and catch it all on hidden cameras. Wait till their husbands find out!*

I turn off my speakers and pull up a video file. Damon is doing Jessie doggie-style, gleefully mauling her cheeks. I gotta admit, she looks good.

CHAPTER 6

Two weeks go by without the usual bead-shop rendezvous. By the third, I figure it's time for me and Kelly to have a chat about Damon. I am just cowardly enough to wait until Jessie finds out about *Horny Housewives* on her own, but I'd like some information should the recriminations come.

I give a three-fingered Boy Scout salute to Marty—who still can't look me in the eye—and fetch my noble 21-speed from the back lot. It's getting dark, and a light rain is falling. As I roll by the entry towers on Palm Drive, a passing image begins to gain detail on my internal screen: a hunched figure in a yellow slicker, the kind you might see on a package of frozen fish. Only, the hands and feet are made of bronze, with rough, exaggerated knuckles.

I'm almost to The El Camino when I realize that the figure is Lisa Pisarro. I stop and swivel my bike around, then chug back to the towers and slide to a rain-hindered halt. I'm only five feet away, but still it's a half-minute before the hood crumples back and the face appears. The readable features have been worn to a Zen-like blank, long days full of grief. She greets me with a nod.

"Mr. Grinder."

"Ms. Pisarro."

"Wheeling into town for baguettes?"

"Oui, mademoiselle."

"You have a stripe like a skunk."

It occurs to me that she might say anything—though she's right, my rear tire has painted my windbreaker with a banner of wet.

"May I sit with you?"

Her eyes flicker, as if she has forgotten and remembered me in the same second.

"Will you do all the talking?"

"Love to."

"I thought you might."

I settle my bike against the tower, then lower myself to the bench, bracing for the small puddles that will further soak my jeans. We sit for a while, facing forward, small rainclouds disassembling themselves over the Stanford shopping mall. I guess I'm waiting for a starter's gun.

"So," she says. "Whattya got?"

"My son continues to surprise the hell out of me. He's decided to take up baseball. And I have no idea what you did to his shoulder, but he seems to have a 93-mile-per-hour fastball. Frankly, it's got all the other kids petrified."

She isn't close to laughing, but she shifts her eyes like she's thinking about it.

"Let's see…The tumor study isn't that far along, but we are beginning to see some interesting patterns. For one thing, the…"

She fixes me with a look of scorn. "I am a woman in desperate need of distraction—and you're talking shop? The Nolan Ryan shoulder thing—that was good. Gimme some more."

"Okay. I'm concerned about my daughter, Laura. She's swimming so much that she's developed webbing between her fingers and toes. She's also sprouted a couple of gills just below her ribcage, and a dorsal fin. It's improved her times tremendously, but if she turns completely to water-breathing, I'm not sure if we can afford the tank."

I consider this to be top-level bullshitting, but Pisarro is looking away, as if she hasn't heard a word. I proceed, regardless.

"My mistress, who likes to paint hookers' faces on her ass, introduced me to a rich geek who seduces bored housewives for a hobby. He agreed to sleep with my wife so she would stop trying to slice out my eyeballs. Turns out he took a video of the whole thing, and now she's on a porn site called 'Horny Housewives.'"

Pisarro turns to me and smiles. Not a big smile, but it's more than I expected.

"Jesus, Hopkins. I wanted amusing stories, not sick fantasies."

I could have told her more. Like the way I've been masturbating to videos of my own wife. Instead, I neutralize the whole subject with, "Well, there ya go."

She gives me her profile again, back to the road, the palm trees, the mountains. Her life is in the distance. A van whips by, leaving the faint smell of coffee. I lift my arm to the back of the bench, grazing Pisarro's shoulder, and turn in the same direction. Five minutes later, I state the inevitable.

"He's gone."
"Yes."

CHAPTER 7

I can't explain this. My wife is on her fifth installment of *Horny Housewives*, and has sprouted a tattoo. It bridges her lower back—favored spot of twenty-somethings—and reads *Cantinflas*, in smooth Gothic lettering.

But here's the catch: it's not really there. Even a man who's not using his husbandly privileges gets occasional glimpses, and believe me—it's not there. So what does *Cantinflas* mean, and how is it arriving? Temporary tattoo? Computer enhancement? It's much too late to be saying so, but this is getting weird.

Otherwise, our lives are nearing perfection. My wife has piled the porch with gourds and pumpkins, and dangled a full-size witch from the magnolia tree. She's also volunteering for a local theater group, taking tickets and selling refreshments.

Marcus is fulfilling every fatherhood fantasy of my generation by following the baseball playoffs with the intensity of an archaeologist charting Atlantis. I'm trying to curb my enthusiasm—lest he dump the whole thing in the coming years of teen rebellion—but when your son asks you how to calculate on-base percentage, it's hard not to break out in tears.

Laura's been taking piano lessons, but was watching a documentary on Yo-Yo Ma and fell in love with the cello. She quotes the master's line about the sound being the closest, of all instruments, to the human voice. We've promised to deliver said instrument on her next birthday, as long as she continues with piano till then.

Perhaps it is exactly this Norman Rockwell/Frank Capra/Walt Disney shit that explains my good behavior. My libido lies in zero-Kelvin stasis, stunned into submission by my good fortune. I do not miss Kelly at all, and have

32   Double Blind

decided that any meeting—even for the sake of porno investigation—would be a bad idea.

Lastly, there is Pisarro. Hopkins Grinder, the man who fucked up his marriage before it started, is now grief counselor to a woman with a soul the size of three football fields. We meet for lunch in the Stanford union, and she tells me stories about Andrew.

He was quite a man. He earned an MBA just so he could run a food bank in Oakland, constructing channels between day-old goods and those who might otherwise be feeding from Dumpsters. He became a leading light of East Bay charities, and was constantly turning down offers to run for office.

Which made it all the more stunning when he went so completely bad. After six months of increasing apathy and ill temper, he walked out of his office one day and never came back. When his family tracked him down, three months later, he was squatting in an abandoned cabin in the Sierra foothills, drinking himself into daily stupors and avoiding all contact with the human race.

"He was always such a rational kid," said Pisarro. "He believed that every problem had a logical solution. Which is why it was so hard for him to understand that he could no longer trust his own mind—that something so trivial as a chemical fluctuation could undo his thoughts."

Pisarro went up there twice, and twice was rebuffed. The second time, he chased her into the road and threw a whiskey bottle that grazed her head. Realizing that Andrew was now a danger to others, she alerted the local sheriff—an action that saved her brother's life. It was on a patrol of the "nutcase cabin" that a deputy discovered him face-down in the driveway, overdosed on sleeping pills.

They locked him up in a mental ward at the county hospital, and Pisarro filed for power of attorney. A month later, she got the news. Andrew had ripped away the corner of a heating vent—tearing his fingers to shreds—and taken the sharp edge to his jugular. Even with regular room-checks, by the time they found him it was too late.

It could be that I'm in love with Pisarro. I'm not sure that it matters. Her sadness gives me something to believe in. I also get a nice tradeoff on sordid details (it's such a relief to tell *someone*!). In fact, she finds my recent escapades so entertaining that it makes me rethink the entire gender. But then, she's a doctor. She's seen everything, and understands sex at its primal level: this enormously pleasurable act that our bodies are designed to perform.

Okay. Don't place me on the rolls of the celibate just yet. I still enjoy watching Dr. Pisarro walk away, and have composed a lengthy to-do list should the heavens grant me her favors. But first things first.

Late at night, when morning has become a distinct possibility, I am dreaming of Pisarro's lips on mine, petals of spongy flesh sliding across my mouth. I seem to think that this is the extent of it—the basic teenage makeout session—but then I feel a distinct warmth surrounding my cock. Am I fucking Pisarro?

The edge of a tooth triggers me awake. My wife is sucking on my dick like it's a circus toy, performing feats of circumlocution that I never dreamed were in her repertoire. She whips her tongue like a tentacle around the head as she works a fist up and down the base. Charged up by weeks of inactivity, I am gone quickly, erupting into her mouth. She swallows, licks me clean, then pulls up beside me with a grin.

"Hi."

"Um…hi," I respond. "Thanks."

"Hoppy? I'm…I'm sorry."

"Whatever for?"

"I've had the chance to…think about things lately, and I think I've spent way too much time blaming you for the way our…intimacies have waned. Desire comes and goes. It's perfectly natural for a marriage to have some dry years. Maybe instead of spending so much energy fighting you, I should have waited for moments like tonight—that delicious hard-on you were dreaming up—and just had my way with you."

I am speechless, and sleepy, and deprived of semen. The most I can do is nod my head. "Sure. Yeah."

She kisses me, open-lipped, and runs her tongue along my teeth. She has never done this before. She backs off and smiles.

"And we made some incredible kids." She laughs. "I'm sorry, honey. You go back to sleep. I'm going to get some water."

She rises and slips into the gray spaces of the hallway. I bury the side of my face in a pillow and reenter the portals of sleep. I am leaning on a split-rail fence beneath snow-tipped volcanic mountains. Pisarro saunters up on a black horse and grants me the easiest smile on the West Coast.

"You're really fucked now, Mr. Grinder. You're beginning to like your wife."

CHAPTER 8

❀

Cantinflas was a popular Mexican comedian (1911–93), a.k.a. Mario Moreno. I looked him up on the web, and found a commentary on a seventies animated series that used his likeness.

The theme was time-travel, but without a time-travel device. Cantinflas just sort of floated through the centuries, meeting famous people, getting into scrapes, messing with the course of history. The comedian's bawdy humor was on full display—including topless women, although for the sake of the kiddies their nipples had been erased.

Pisarro bursts into laughter. "Nipple erasure? Ouch!"

"And still, the essential question," I continue. "What is he doing on my wife's ass?"

I have come to the conclusion that Pisarro is the only person in the world to whom I can tell absolutely everything. We sit at a table behind the union, one of those sunny late-October days, crisp and bright as the first bite of an apple.

I spy a figure descending a slope of lawn—thin, professorial, no surprise except that it's Richard Zwei. I rise to greet him with a handshake.

"Dad! How the hell did you find me here?"

He seems a little on-edge—but, as usual, fully capable of charming his way through it.

"Your habits are well known at the lab," he reports. "And a lawyer—even a retired one—knows how to finagle information."

"Dad, this is Dr. Lisa Pisarro, the woman who so nicely reassembled Marcus's shoulder. Pisarro, this is my father-in-law, Richard Zwei."

"My pleasure," he says, and takes Pisarro's hand. "I hope I'm not being a bother, but could I steal Hopkins away for a minute?"

"As a matter of fact, I need to leave, anyway. We're a little short on staff today."

She gathers her purse and gives me the customary hug. Richard and I watch her go. I'm expecting some wry comment about her figure, but in fact he's only making certain that she's out of earshot. He sits at the table, hunching in an uncharacteristic way, and rubs his eyes.

I pretend to show some interest in my Coke. "What's up, Dad?"

He looks at me and lets out a half-sigh.

"Hop, I never was much with computers. Avoided using them for years—but then I saw how much the grandkids liked 'em, so I figured it was a good way to keep in touch."

Most of what follows gets lost in the race of my thoughts. I have several scripts for this same conversation with Jessie, but what do you tell the father of the bride?

"…and there she is, spread out in her birthday suit, boinking some strange man. We did some racy things in my day, Hopkins, but we didn't broadcast it to the world!"

He places a palm on either side of his face and looks to me for a reaction. I'm working on selective honesty.

"I know about this, Dad."

His eyebrows elevate. "And…have you…done anything?"

"No. I'm sort of stuck."

He rubs a hand over his mouth. "Jesus, Hop. Have the rules changed that much? Aren't you supposed to find this guy and kick his ass? Aren't you supposed to…have it out with Jessie? For God's sake, aren't you even pissed off?"

"I've been…having an affair, too. And there's something else. You remember when I had those stitches under my eye?"

"Jessie did that?"

"Yeah. Maybe on purpose, maybe not. But she was so frantic, she was getting dangerous. I was worried about the kids. When Jessie got better, and I found out about the porn site, I guess it seemed like a fair trade. Also, this way, at least I know that she's using condoms."

I stop as a group of Indian students walk by, armed with Frisbees.

"I guess you know this, Dad, but Jessie and I have had some rough years."

Richard kneads his forehead, trying to process ideas he never thought he'd have to deal with in his lifetime. It's really unfair, the load of changes we have foisted on this particular generation of men. They were told only to work, and provide for their families, and the rest would come out in the wash.

"I've had a couple of flings myself," he says. "I suppose you might've guessed, what with the gigantic broomstick crammed up my wife's bee-hind. I'd like to say I regretted them—but I'm not fond of perjury. Those dear women got me through some very trying times."

"What can I do for you, Hop? Can I protect you somehow? I've seen how men get shafted in divorce courts."

"Dad, I honestly don't care. I'll be okay. But if things do get out of hand, could you keep an eye out for Laura and Marcus?"

He draws a finger over his mustache. "Sure, Hop. That I will."

CHAPTER 9

I'm picking up Marcus from school. I forget why. An email from Jessie. I skipped out of work early.

Maybe it's the bully. She said something about a bully. The parking lot is empty, so I get out and wander into the courtyard. Marcus is perched on a bench, calm as a Buddha, while some little black cub dances around him like a boxer, slapping the top of Marcus's head as he peels off insults.

"Big ol' fagboy, that's all y'are, jus' love a big ol' cock up your asshole. Makes ya drool, gives you a boner jus' thinkin' 'bout that cock. What? Now it's in your mouth? Mmmm, tastes good! Whatsamatter? Can't fight back? Lookit ol' Queen Marcus, gonna move to San Francisco and die of AIDS, little ol' dick gonna break in two and fall right off. Poor ol' fagboy."

He goes in for another slap but falls short when I grab his wrist and yank it behind his back. I grip his opposite shoulder for leverage and dig a knee into his spine. I could break him, right now.

"What's your name, kid?"

"Ponce."

"Like the explorer?"

"Y-yeah."

He's scared shitless, the little bastard.

"That's good," I say. "Now, number one, the only reason my son hasn't pounded your little black ass into pudding is that I promised his parole officer I'd keep him on a short leash. The last little boy who taunted him just got out of the hospital, and so far he can say 'hello,' 'cat' and 'wa-wa.'

"Number two: 'Fagboy?' That's the best you can do? Jesus, they were telling fag jokes when I was a kid. Besides, have you noticed who's runnin' Hollywood

38   Double Blind

these days? Now. I'm gonna let you go, and I want you outta my sight quick, or I and my pit-bull son will be on your sorry ass like ugly on your mama. Okay?"

He says nothing.

"Okay?" I repeat.

"Y-yeh. Sure."

I shove him forward. He stumbles to his knees, then scrambles up and takes off like a shot. He stops at the corner, however, 'cause he just can't help himself.

"Cocksucker!"

"Oh, *very* original!" I reply. I turn to Marcus, who looks horrified. "What's your problem?"

"You're making it worse, Dad. Now he's gonna think I'm a big wuss."

"Well maybe you are! I've had it with your goddamn pacifism, Mahatma. The next time little Ponce gives you any shit, you are under direct orders to push his punk ass to the ground. They're not gonna leave you alone until you *do* something, Marcus. I'm sorry, but that's the way the world works."

I head for the car and hear Marcus plodding behind me. I am a bad father. I am dispensing questionable advice.

Driving home, I think of Robert Mapplethorpe, that photographer who caused all the fuss in the eighties. One of his shots was a self-portrait, the artist squatting nude, a bullwhip trailing behind him like a tail—the handle stuck up his ass. I first saw it in a gallery in San Francisco. After the initial shock, it made perfect sense. Christians had taken a single physical act—the insertion of an object into a man's rectum—and labeled it the work of Satan. With his devil's tail, Mapplethorpe was simply acting out the crime.

Another showed a dark black man and a pale white man in a nude embrace. Remove the societal subtext, note the sharp focus, and you have an aesthetically intriguing study in contrast: black and white skin in a black and white shot. Sadly, I know few minds agile enough to make that separation. Perhaps F. Scott Fitzgerald. Perhaps Pisarro.

This morning, I got in early to work and pulled up *Horny Housewives*. Cantinflas on my wife's shoulder. A large black cock up her ass.

This is not all. At lunch, I found myself wandering downtown, a nameless ache in my throat, my limbs insufferably light. I spotted a bright sign in a sushi bar and my brain emptied out—water down a drain. I have felt this before, but so long ago I cannot name it.

I pull into the driveway. Jessie's in the side yard, attacking the lemon tree. Her latest domestic obsession. Lemon tarts, lemon meringue pie, lemon poppyseed muffins. I open the door and swing out my legs. She smiles.

"Hi dear. Would you like some lemonade?"

"Sure, honey. That sounds great."

(Dear? Honey? Whose house is this?)

"Marcus?" she says. "Would you…?"

Marcus is gone, up the walk.

"Is he all right?"

"Rough day," I reply.

She twists her lip. "The bully?"

"Yep."

"Oh dear."

"Don't worry—it'll be okay."

"Poor Marc. He's got so many feelers, he's bound to get them bruised."

We enter the house. My wife pours me a lemonade. I watch a Disney cartoon with my daughter. The strange feeling, the lightness in my limbs, fades away.

The next day, my greeting is not so warm. Jessie storms down the walk, her hair tangled, teeth pressed together in a hiss.

"What the hell were you thinking?! You can't go around assaulting other people's kids. He's a twelve-year-old, for Chrissake! Are you trying to get thrown into jail? Are you trying to turn your son into a monster?"

"Is he okay?"

"Of course not!"

"Ah shit. Is he beat up?"

She looks at me like I'm the biggest idiot in the world.

"Ponce is in the hospital."

I gotta admit, for a second I'm enjoying this. Ponce deserves whatever he gets. But that's not the way my son sees it. When I get to his room, he's got a Spiderman website on his computer screen, but he's not really looking. When I put a hand on his shoulder, he speaks in a low, crackling tone.

"I did what you said, Dad. I pushed him. But we were right next to this railing…"

He looks at me with moist eyes that could slay a devil.

"He wasn't moving, Dad. I thought he was dead. I thought I killed him."

I squat next to his chair and wrap a hand at the back of his neck, riding out his tears, taking my punishment.

CHAPTER 10

Stanford has a lake, Lake Lagunita, which translates as "Lake Small Lagoon." This makes about as much sense as "The El Camino"—particularly because Lake Lagunita is hardly ever a lake. The winter rainfall offers enough water for a few weeks of sailboarding, but the rest of the year it's dry. It used to be the site for the bonfire before the Big Game against Cal, but then they discovered it was the breeding ground for endangered California tiger salamanders, and decided to give the poor buggers some peace.

When Pisarro requested a ghost-lake picnic, I didn't much see the point, but she did have a nice spot picked out: a bench at the northwest corner, in the shade of a live oak. The branches sprawl out in that gnarly, witchy fashion, dropping acorns that land at our feet with leafy smacks.

We've just settled in, performed our usual huggy greeting, when a man comes loping toward us in a suit and tie.

"Hi! God, long time. How you been?"

I'm preparing a fake, nameless greeting when the man looks sideways, revealing the telephone hookup in his ear. He proceeds down the trail, yapping away.

"Pisarro, ten years ago that man would've been locked up."

She looks at me and laughs. She's beautiful. She's back to wearing makeup, a further sign of recovery. The dark lipstick and purple eyeshadow bestow magic on her Mediterranean features. I hope some of this effort is for me. The longings grow by the day—the dry mouth, the trains of thought that scatter like cockroaches—and Dr. Pisarro is a prime suspect.

"What *are* you thinking about?" she says.

Michael J. Vaughn 41

She's looking at me sideways, opening up the white acres beside her irises. This does things to me.

"Tiger salamanders," I reply.

"They're beautiful. I saw one once when I was hiking." She smiles. "So tell me about your son the ruffian."

"Man! What was I thinking? Our friend Ponce came out okay—just a concussion, though they did have to keep an eye on him. You know."

"Yes, I do."

"Marcus has a spotless record. Had. So they let him off easy. Two days' suspension. Eight hours' volunteer work. I'm surprised he didn't ask for more."

"Lots of guilt?"

"Oh yeah. You could give that kid a separated shoulder, broken bones, migraine headaches—no problem. But make him visit suffering on someone else…"

She peers across the lakebed, where cars are buzzing by on the expressway. "I'm imagining what any other kid would say. 'He was asking for it.' 'It was an accident.' 'My dad made me do it.'"

"Not the Mea Culpa Kid. When I'm not picturing him getting eaten alive out there, I am amazed at his compassion."

Pisarro raises a toast with her ginger ale. "Marcus, the Peacemaker." Then she settles her head to the back of the bench and closes her eyes. "God, I really needed to come out here. Work has been so crazy. It's like they…"

The rest goes right past me. One of Pisarro's blouse buttons has popped open. I can see the top of her breast, a pliable tan plumpness lipping out over a lacy black bra. The caustic lightness burns through my limbs and I am reaching across, slipping through the narrow gap of fabric as my hand settles on her nipple.

Followed by pain. She grips my wrist, digging in with her nails as she pushes it away like a small but dangerous animal. Then she slouches forward, gripping her legs, oddly silent.

"Shit!"

It comes out as a short hiss, air brakes on a bus. Pisarro jumps up and walks away. I am left on a bench with two sack lunches. Once again the fuckup.

My judgement is so far off, I'm afraid to go to work. I'm afraid of the damage I could inflict on our study. I stroll carefully to the front lawn, where the bright weather has caused an outbreak of volleyball. I park myself on a bench, settle the two lunches next to me and stare into a bed of pansies until the purple bleeds into a solid square.

Perhaps I have picked a bad spot. Some of the girls are well endowed. And volleyball is a vertical sport.

"Excuse me."

She catches me by surprise.

"Could you tell me where Kresge Auditorium is?"

The following inventory takes half a second: coffee skin (heavy on the cream); wide, plush lips with a sharp cupid's bow on the upper; eyes like black olives behind thin-framed glasses (got a thing about glasses), and a thick mane of black ringlets, falling past her shoulders like a shawl. Time's up.

"Sure," I reply. "Do you have a piece of paper?"

She hands me a steno pad, and I draw a map. She sits beside me to watch. She's wearing a white cotton dress with petticoats—crosses her legs to reveal brown leather boots (got a thing about boots). I hand her the pad.

"So immaculate!" She's got an accent that's hard to locate: Carolina, Bronx. Long vowels.

"I'm a scientist," I say. "I like to get things right."

"Oh!" She smiles. "Do you work here on campus?"

"Yes, I do."

"I'm interviewing for a job with the lively arts program. Thought I should scope out the performance spaces. Is it nice working here?"

A tall Japanese man fires a spike at one of the well-endowed girls, driving her backward.

"Really nice. It used to be weird, being around all these students. But they're great kids—intensely curious. I think I feed off of that."

She lowers her voice. "Is it any problem…if you just got your master's at Berkeley?"

"You are speaking to a Golden Bear at this very moment."

"Really!" She laughs. "Is it tough, being in enemy territory?"

"You will find, after a few red-and-white paychecks, that your loyalties tend to wander."

She opens her mouth in mock horror. "Never!" Then turns to watch the volleyball match, revealing a golden stud in the side of her nose. I have a thing for this, also. How have all these tremendous parts come together in this one package?

"My father is Jewish, and my mother is from Kenya." She answers my look with a grin. "You held out longer than most. Next answer. Nef. N-E-F. Now! If you can guess…"

"Nefertiti."

"My!" she says (this from Carolina). "You just won a cuppa java."

"I…did?"

"That's what I was going to offer before you so rudely cut me off."

"Oh." I feel like a schoolboy, unsure of my words. "I…Don't you have to see the auditorium?"

She holds up two fingers, like a witch casting a spell, and taps them on my shoulder. "Much better to pick the brain of an authentic Stanford scientist."

We end up in town, at the University Café. It occurs to me that this is where I first met Kelly. I'm hoping there's something in the coffee here, because I desperately want to fuck this woman. It's crowded, so she tells me to save a table while she orders our drinks. She walks away with that fashion-model twist, one foot directly before the other. The cotton dress sways, as do the generous hips.

Perhaps this is the key to my unexplained longings. Typical of a scientist, I have lost myself in overwrought hypotheses, and overlooked the obvious. After two years of steady, illicit sex with Kelly, I have gone two months without. I am a randy little salamander, and my needs are not being met. Nef returns with cappuccinos; hers has a sprinkling of chocolate.

When we leave, a half-hour later, she spots the marquee of the Stanford Theater.

"The Thin Man! Oh my God! Myrna Loy is my goddess."

"So let's go," I say.

"Don't you have to go back to work?"

"I have no idea." I also have no idea if I'm supposed to pick up a child somewhere, be home for dinner, drop my wife's car at the garage. This is Tuesday afternoon, spun gold, and I desperately want to collect.

Nef takes my hand and leads me into the theater. When the movie starts, she leans her head against my shoulder; the black ringlets tickle my jawline. When William Powell takes Myrna in a clinch, Nef turns to kiss me on the cheek. As the credits roll, she whispers an invitation. I am aloft in a blur of yes.

I remember very little. I am flat on a bed, naked, morning light silking in through the blinds. I hear the rivery whoosh of the freeway, am awake but exhausted, consumed by an image: Nefertiti, mounted on my cock like a trophy, using her hips to perform feats of kinetic geometry. She still has her glasses on.

I roll to the edge of the bed and rub my eyes. I'm awfully thirsty. I stumble to the sink, my feet like uncooperative frogs, and unwrap one of those plastic motel cups. When I reach for the tap, I find writing on the mirror, pink lipstick, big looping letters.

Hi Hopkins. Thanks for a great night! By the way, I'm 16.

—Nef

CHAPTER 11

The ichneumon wasp provides for its progeny by injecting its eggs into the body of a caterpillar. When the eggs hatch, the ichneumon larvae begin eating their host from the inside out—taking great care to preserve the heart and central nervous system, so as to keep their victim alive (and fresh) as long as possible.

"Finally," writes scientist/essayist Stephen Jay Gould, "the larva completes its work and kills its victims, leaving behind the caterpillar's empty shell. Is it any wonder that ichneumons, not snakes or lions, stood as the paramount challenge to God's benevolence during the heyday of natural theology?"

I am the criminal with no accuser, the man afire among people who refuse to see flames. I walked three miles from the motel to the lab, wearing the same clothes as the day before. Nobody noticed. I came home. Jessie said nothing; she smiled and poured me a lemonade. I'm dying to know how she explained my absence to the kids, but I didn't dare ask.

Because I fucked a girl four years older than Marcus.

I walk with a cloud of gnats about my head, bedeviled by motives and menace. Blackmail? I would have received a demand. Revenge? I picture Nefertiti raped by her stepfather, reaping karmic retribution through any man his age. But she seemed too…together for this.

I'm at my desk, making entries in next week's schedule, when two observable facts announce their presence. One: the University Café. Two: Tuesday afternoon. Conclusion: Kelly.

At lunchtime, I hop on my bike and follow the old route to the bead shop. I open the door, the bells jangle, and I am pleased (finally!) to get a response

46   Double Blind

from someone. Kelly's eyes grow wide; she tightens her grip on the edge of the counter. I approach at a measured pace and speak the only word I can think of.

"Nefertiti."

Kelly blinks her lashes theatrically. "Nice to see you, too. What the *hell* do you want?"

I take a jade ring from a basket and balance it on my pinkie.

"You don't know what 'Nefertiti' means."

"Foggiest, darling. Egyptian queen?"

"You didn't set me up?"

"Are you still on this shit? Jesus! So my son was on the same five acres when you nailed me on a putting green. Get over it! Why are you even here, Hopkins? Are you horny, is that why you're here? Because, at the moment, I'm having a regular and satisfying relationship with a big pink plastic dildo!"

The door jangles open. Kelly smiles.

"Why do they always come in on a word like 'dildo'?"

A fiftyish woman with fiercely perfect blonde hair arrives at the counter.

"I've got these linen pants with a sleeveless top—sort of orange and brown, safari colors, very Kenya—and I'm looking for something dramatic to set it off. Maybe a pendant."

Kelly takes her to a corner with African masks and jewelry, leaving me at the counter, trying to rattle my brain into the present reality.

One: Kelly's look of surprise was genuine. Two: no response at all to the name "Nefertiti." Three: total misinterpretation as to the meaning of my visit. Four: if I go so far as to explain who Nefertiti is, I have just created a witness where previously there were none.

I slip out the door, a phantom afire, and am soon rolling above The El Camino, headed for the safety of my laboratory. Disparage the scientist all you want, but he is well equipped to understand when he is wrong, and when to abandon a lost cause.

At the end of the afternoon, the name *Pisarro* appears on my email.

Hopkins—

Call me a weak woman, but I received the following this morning, and I can't imagine that they came from you. Fun is fun, but what the hell are you getting yourself into?

Please don't answer this. After the other day, I'm going to need some time before I trust you again.

What follows—a forwarded email—comes from an address beginning "Ramses16@…" Attached are several images of myself *in flagrante delicto* with Nefertiti. The subject line reads *Geneticist Fails Carbon Dating*.

Dr. Solenin is a tall, elegant man, Jamaican by birth, who always reminds me of Nelson Mandela. He works in the administrative building across campus, and almost never visits the lab. When he does, it's noteworthy.

"Dr. Solenin!" I pivot from my chair and greet him with a handshake. "What brings you here?"

He studies his hands, looking anxious. "It's not good, Hopkins. Please. Follow me."

He leads me down the hall to Marty's office. Marty is gone. Solenin sits at Marty's desk and waves me into a chair. The blood is thrumming through my head. I'm trying to formulate an appropriate reaction: one-half concern, one-half shock, followed by a simmering indignation.

"It's about your drug test."

Or confusion—that I can do.

"The one you took Wednesday," he says. "It indicated the presence of MDMA."

MDMA? What the…?

"Ecstasy?" I say.

He nods, and leans forward on the desk.

"Here's how it goes from here. You need to report back to the testing center this afternoon—within the hour, actually, before it closes. If this test confirms the positive, you will be suspended without pay until the personnel committee can meet to discuss your situation. I'm very sorry."

CHAPTER 12

I leave the testing center, knowing that I will fail. My memories of Tuesday are like figures viewed through marbled glass, but a few odd tracks are clear. Nefertiti found an excuse for buying me a drink—then, arriving at a busy café, instructed me to save a table while she got the cappuccinos. She sprinkled hers with chocolate, mine with Ecstasy. God knows why. Considering my state of mind—and her lustworthy attributes—why would she need chemical assistance?

It's a crisp autumn day, clouds jogging across the sky like portly triathletes. I'm driving Bryant Street, where the town squires have blocked off the avenue at regular intervals, and inserted narrow bridges so only bikes and pedestrians can get through. I take great pleasure in living in a place where they actually think of such things. Or perhaps I am desperate for positives. A quintet of cyclists passes me the other way in their European silks, like grimly determined tropical birds. I turn left into Mrs. Brendel's driveway.

My lovely daughter meets me at the door. Her T-shirt features a baroque composer in Schwarzenegger sunglasses and the words *I'll Be Bach*.

"Heya, dishalish."

"Hi, Dadsalish." She turns back toward the living room. "Bye, Mrs. Brendel!"

"Bye, honey! Remember—posture!"

"Posture!" she says, giggling.

I can hold back no longer. I grab her under the arms and swing her into the air. Songsheets go flying.

"Dadsalish!" she scolds. We scurry across the yard, picking pages from the boxwood. "You must be more careful!"

This makes me laugh for a good long time. Realizing how witty she has been, Laura drops her show of disapproval for a self-satisfied smile. When she ducks under a rose bush after *Für Elise*, I slip a couple of fallen leaves into her music folder. We're halfway home, sitting at a backed-up intersection, when she discovers my sabotage.

"Dadsalish!" She takes the leaves in either hand—a red and a yellow—and makes them dance like puppets.

"Are you leafing through your music, Lauralish?"

"Oh!" She takes an invisible arrow to the shoulder. (I have told her that puns are dangerous things, and she has taken it to a logical, nine-year-old extreme.) "Dadsalish! That's bad."

"Would you like me to leaf the subject alone?"

"Aigh!" The other shoulder.

"You autumn not fall for such tricks."

"Gah!" The stomach.

"I used to be uncertain about such matters, but now I'm deciduous."

She opens one eye to peer at me quizzically.

"Yes, it's a pun," I explain.

"Eeh!" Straight through the heart, and she slumps backward, holding the leaves over her chest like lilies.

"Howl! Howl! Howl!" I lament, drawing on my scant Shakespeare. "I have slain sweet Cordelia with my savage punnery."

The corpse returns to life and whacks me on the shoulder.

"Get thee to a punnery!"

"Gack!" I take an arrow in the neck. But the light turns green, so I heal quickly. Laura gives her leaves a closer study.

"What are these from, Dadsalish?"

"Gimme." She puts them in my hand, and I peek while dodging cars.

"The yellow's a birch, and the red's…an Oregon maple."

She takes them back and holds them next to each other as if they're having a conversation.

"Mrs. Schmidt says that leaves are sun-harvesters, and to do their work they put on green jackets. Chlor…chloro…"

"Phyll," I say. "Chlorophyll."

"Yeah! But in the fall, when it gets cold, the leaves take off their work clothes, and yellow is their real color. And the tree can't support them anymore, so it lets them fall to the ground. And that's why they call it 'fall.'"

"You are a brilliant child," I say. "Where did you get all these brains?"

"From Dadsalish."

"And Machiavellian, as well."

"Huh?"

"And observant, as well. But…what about the red leaves?"

"Umm…" She runs the maple across her lips, willing it to give up its secrets. "Oh! She says they're not sure, but the red might be a way for the leaf to send as much sun as it can to the tree before it falls off. It's kind of a…panic attack."

"Or a red alert," I say. Laura giggles.

We cruise the last two miles in silence. Laura, my daughter who makes Hamlet jokes, is scouring the yards and strip malls for red and yellow trees.

It occurs to me that I'm a big fat liar. I've told that story about failing my medical exam for so long that I believed it myself. It wasn't to spite my mother; it wasn't to avoid dealing with people. I failed that exam because I wanted to be a scientist, I wanted to poke and prod the giant quizbox of nature and make her give up her secrets. But not all of them, because I wanted the game to go on forever.

Now, nature has tricked me. I am a big red maple leaf, about to be dropped from the tree.

The morning that follows, I see the kids off, kiss the wife on the cheek, and make a show of driving off to work. Once free of the neighborhood, I loop around to a copy shop to check my email, and I receive the expected news: the MDMA is a confirmed resident of my bloodstream, and I am not welcome at the lab.

I give serious consideration to a day at the beach, but figure I'd better stay within a ten-mile radius of Stanford, where a chance sighting would raise no alarms. Be it horny housewife, statutory rape or unintentional drug abuse, I am back in my customary position, guilty of crimes I dare not speak. I miss Pisarro.

I'm cruising The El Camino, fiddling with the radio, when I land on some techno thing, a chocolate pudding of beeps and bloops over a rhythm track that sounds like a thousand chopsticks whapping a granite slab. It's oddly refreshing (or perhaps I am desperate for positives). I am sinking into the trance when a woman cuts in with a deep, placid voice—the kind you might expect of a psychologist, or dominatrix.

"That *thing* was 'Na Na Neurons' by the Contra Tempos, a little splash from ought-one. Preceded by 'Bugarilla' from Hans Offal. You're on the Morning Buzz Saw with Ann Apolis, a half-hour away from Paulie Unsaturated and his

Punkalollabrigida. I'll be back with a few more doses of pulsation after these messages from the dark overlords of KFJC Radio, Foothill College."

She switches to a pre-recorded plug for the holiday theater show. I take a left onto Castro, looking for a pool hall. At the corner of Mercy Street, Ann Apolis returns.

"Don't forget the Foothill Ski Club's annual venture to Heavenly Valley, December six. Take it from a wily veteran—the skiing is much better if you've got a big audience for your crash-and-burn stories."

I take a U-turn and head for the college.

Two years before, Jessie and I were herding the kids to that same holiday show when Laura spotted a woman in the window. When the woman spoke, her words came out of a speaker in front of the building.

"Wow!" she said. "How cool is that?"

I park at a far lot and try to recall the route, up through a Japanese garden, past a natural-wood classroom complex, a trio of squat brick buildings on the left. The entrance is unmistakable, a cluttered lobby of old furniture and underground concert posters. A nerdish kid in a green sweater-vest sits in a fuzzy armchair, drilling in on a calculus textbook.

"Hi," I say. "Is Ann Apolis almost off?"

He finishes a line and checks his watch. "Yes. She's off in…Cripes!"

He scrambles for the back hall, leaving me mouthing the word "Cripes?"

Seconds later, I hear an angry person with a British accent, snarling an intro for the Dead Kennedys. A woman appears in the doorway, pleasantly rotund, with leonine blonde hair, blue-gray eyes and a beauty-queen smile.

"Hopkins?"

"Nancy," I say. "Nancy Bloomsburg."

We sit in the quad beneath a squadron of sprawling non-Oregon maples, sprinkling us with leather-brown leaves (Laura would love it). I'm down to the final pocket on a plastic photo-holder.

"That's our youngest, Kyle. Little opera star, that one. When he wants my attention, he sings, 'Mom-mee!' I swear, someday he's gonna break glass."

"Four boys! You must feel like you're living in a locker room."

"Suits me fine. I'm a total tomboy, anyway."

"Definitely."

We share an awkward pause—after 15 years, it's expected. A leaf strikes my knee, its sides crinkled up like a tiny coracle.

"So where'd you get 'Ann Apolis'?"

52   Double Blind

She laughs with that lovely whiskey edge. "Well, I'm from Maryland. And the wacky pseudonym is unofficial station policy. Wouldn't do if people found out their techno chick was a bovine mother of four."

"Or that Paulie Unsaturated is...whatever he is."

She slaps the bench. "I know! I can't even watch him work, or I absolutely lose it. I just want to spank him and send him home to his mother."

We laugh until we're both looking away, at the maple-leaf ceiling.

"I got laid off by National Semi a couple years ago—and Frank's job was doing well—so I thought, by damn, it's time to live out the old DJ fantasy. Foothill's absolutely the best."

"So I've heard."

"What about you? What the hell are you up to?"

She is just the confidante I've been looking for, but there are minefields everywhere.

"It's been tough, Nancy—especially lately. But we're working on it."

She touches my knee. "Don't think Frank and I haven't had our stretches."

"That's marriage." I'm sinking into cliché. And there's something I want out of this. Nancy is gathering up her purse, and about to say something like, *Well, I've really got to...*

"Nancy? Do you remember when we broke up?"

She stops cold, and studies my face. "It was the most horrible thing I've ever done in my life."

Now *I'm* taken aback.

"Really?"

She looks at the grass, then squints her eyes like she's getting a headache. This is an old expression. It means she's trying to get something just right.

"Schroeder was an old flame from high school. He went back east for college, and was paying his last visit to California before taking a job in Sweden. One last weekend, a little skiing at Squaw—Schroeder's gone and I'm back to you. I wanted to marry you, Hopkins. But old flames...heat up. And college girls make incredibly stupid mistakes. And not even Nancy Bloomsburg had the gall—or the courage—to ask forgiveness for a crime that large."

Fifteen years later, the old story is bringing water to Nancy's eyes. I take her shoulders and kiss her on the cheek.

"Life's pretty astounding."

She laughs. "Damned astounding."

"I'm glad I found you again. You've got my email?"

"And you've got mine."

"But no ski weekends."
"Hah! Certainly not."
"Bye, Nanc."
"Bye, Hopkins."

I circle the big hill of campus and come back out to the freeway, dazed by the vicious reconstructions of chance. If Gunnar doesn't spy Nancy and Schroeder at Squaw Valley, my unhappy marriage is gone. Nancy's four boys. Laura and Marcus, replaced by genetic shadows in the chemical soufflé of love-making.

Acknowledging that I am living in a parallel universe seems to lessen my troubles. Perhaps I'll be all right. Perhaps I think too much. Paulie's playing the Ramones, I'm hitting the gas—the Punkalollabrigida is open for business.

CHAPTER 13

It was a survey of 16,000 American adults, a paper published in 2004 by David G. Blanchflower and Andrew J. Oswald. The finding that made the news was that greater income does not buy more sex, nor more sexual partners. But the finding that surprised me was the "happiness-maximizing" number of sexual partners in the previous year: one.

What I remember is the combination of smells: newmown grass, glove leather and cigarette smoke. Wearing a suede jacket, passing a smoker in the park, I find myself on the Pioneer Little League Twins, crouching at third, praying a bad hop doesn't smack me in my new braces.

All that's missing today are the cigarettes (modern courtesies being what they are), but I do feel twelve years old. I plant a cooler of team refreshments at my wife's feet and settle into the bleachers. Mr. Tomjonowitz exclaims "Play ball!" I'm about to pee my pants.

Marcus has the same dilemma I had, but in the opposite sport. When I was twelve, soccer had just penetrated the American consciousness, and I couldn't do a thing with my feet. Voila! A goalkeeper. In Marcus's case, years of goalkeeping has taught him how to catch a ball, and stop a grounder, but not to throw. Add the minor detail that's he's six feet tall and Voila! A first baseman.

The second batter of the season is a small, determined southpaw who jumps on the first pitch and smashes a grounder down the line. Marcus slides over in front of it, takes a bad hop off his chest, corrals the ball at his feet and races to the bag. His first putout. I grin at my wife.

"Okay. You remember how we practiced?"

I give her the high five, the scissor clinch and the fist bump, followed by the voodoo finger-waggle. We snap our fingers and point at Marcus, who saw our little performance and is cracking up. Any other kid would be mortified.

I'm sorry. Greeting-card moments with the wife? I'm confusing you. Let's back up.

I am the greatest dodger of bullets in American history. For an entire month, I pretended to have a job, shuttling credit card advances to my bank account to impersonate paychecks. When that gave out, I went to Richard with sad stories about stock losses. I asked him not to tell Jessie, because I wanted her and the kids to enjoy the holidays. Having spent years hiding casino losses from his own wife, Richard had his checkbook out before I could say "please." God bless that man.

I spent my days at a pool hall in Mountain View, honing my eight-ball skills with a group of laid-off techies. Meanwhile, I kept up an email correspondence with Marty, who gave me regular updates on the study. He also seeded the lab with a cover story about my ailing uncle in Michigan. Poor Marty was carrying around more illicit info than a Mafia snitch. God bless that man.

Every Tuesday and Thursday, I hiked an open space preserve near Foothill College, my Walkman tuned to Nancy's show. I wasn't ready to drag the woman into my murky present—she had enough on her plate—but it was good to hear her voice, to recall the saffron hopes of my alternate universe.

Nefertiti disappeared. Whatever her motives, they didn't include criminal charges. I was grateful.

In mid-December, the personnel committee met to consider my fate. Citing my devotion to the cause and sterling record, they invited me to return to work after New Year's. They also invited me to attend a weekly meeting of former users. I told Jessie I was attending a networking group for scientists, and reported each Wednesday to a Quaker hall in Palo Alto.

Facing authentic victims of chemistry and addiction, shadowed by the cabernet blur of my mother, I felt enormously humbled. And ashamed—that I should take a life most people would envy and pollute it with cheap drama.

Most of this havoc began with my vagabond penis, so I resolved to tame it. Whenever I could grab a couple hours, I checked into a hotel, rented a prick-flick, and masturbated to my heart's content.

Without, I might add, the help of *Horny Housewives*. My wife's antics had disappeared from the Web. Even the old stuff—yanked out of the archives as if it had never existed. I was tired of trying to figure this out, and more than happy to cultivate a friendship with the real item. Sometimes all you need is

56   Double Blind

the affection that sprouts from a mutual interest, and in our bright, beautiful children, Jessie and I had the best of all possible hobbies.

And God! The kid can hit a ball. He comes up in the third inning, raises that right elbow just like I told him, and strokes a drive over the centerfield fence. Jessie and I forgo the fancy handshake for indecorous screaming.

Marcus is enormously embarrassed by the hullabaloo (a home run being the rudest thing you can do to an opposing pitcher). But he seems to enjoy the mob scene at the plate, teammates gathering to happily pound the snot out of him. The ringleader is his new best friend, Ponce. How boys manage to do that, I'll never know.

"Don't leave any loose ends," says my drug counselor. "Apologize to anyone who has been hurt because of your addiction." Ponce and Marcus remind me of my last untied shoelace. I resolve to take care of it.

When she arrives, I am standing in front of Cybele, an alluring headless woman. Unfortunate choice, but I grew nervous in my waiting, and had to pace. Pisarro approaches at a deliberate rate.

She looks healthy, and thinner, although it takes nothing away from the appealing roundness of her face and eyes. It's a warm day, even for March. She wears a floral dress (magnolia blossoms), and a delicate white sweater, laced at the cuffs. I stand ready as she approaches, fidgeting with her bracelet like a nervous bride. She manages a smile.

"Hi."

"Pisarro. I'm glad you came."

"Um…yes."

"I'm told a white carnation is a good flower for apology." I extend my envoy, the flawless one that looks like a tissue-paper phony. She holds it with both hands.

"Thanks."

I gesture to our old spot near the Shades. She settles on the bench; I remain standing. I dig a foot into the sandy gravel, like Marcus getting ready to bat. I have rehearsed this several times, but I still don't know exactly what will come out of my mouth.

"There were things going on that week. Things I can't explain. I don't mean this as an excuse. I mean this to indicate that this kind of…behavior is unusual for me. Whatever my sexual escapades, I don't generally attack unless I'm invited."

I'm a skier on an icy incline, gathering speed, unsure of where I should cut my blades.

"I hate myself for that day. Your sadness, your love for your brother were…enthralling to me. I didn't know a human soul could run that deep. And you took this fragile part of yourself and shared it with me. I felt…honored. You trusted me so much, and I fucked it up.

"I've learned a lot of humility lately. The hard way—believe me. It's been good. But I need one more thing. I need a chance to win back your trust. I miss your friendship, Pisarro. I miss our lunches. And I miss you."

Here is the old joke: *What women find most attractive in a man is sincerity. Once you learn how to fake that, you've got it made.*

I'm here to tell you: you can't fake it. And one day you might find yourself in a garden of French sculptures, your skin so transparent that people could read roadsigns through your ribcage. And a woman with dewy onyx eyes will walk your way, comb her fingers into your hair, and bestow upon your lips, The Kiss.

Five minutes later, we separate and start laughing. She parts those ripe lips and says, "How 'bout lunch?"

We take her car to the Peninsula Creamery, a nifty old diner in Palo Alto. Pisarro ignores the menu, smiles at the waiter and says five remarkable words: "I'll have the Bubbly Burger."

The Bubbly Burger is a Silicon Valley institution: cheeseburger, fries and a bottle of Dom Perignon for $150.75. In the dot-com nineties, lots of young supernerds would use it to celebrate their latest stock offering.

I stare at Pisarro; she does me the favor of staring back.

"You're one surprise after another," I say.

"Yes. But I do have an explanation."

She stops. I roll one hand forward. "Ye-es?"

She smiles, close-mouthed. "I refuse to talk until I have fine champagne on my lips."

The waiter arrives, wearing a grin, wrestling with the cork. "This is so cool! We don't do so many of these since, you know…"

"The bubble burst?" I say.

"Exactly." The cork pops. He fills Pisarro's glass, and hands me a Coke. She takes the stem and lifts.

"To the new director of the Intensive Care Unit."

"No shit!"

"Please! Drink first, swear later."

I lift my Coke and swallow.

"Congratulations! Does this explain our Rodin rendezvous?"

"Not really."

"I had such good honest Boy Scout intentions, and you mucked it all up."

"Oh dear. And I know that must be a rare moment for you."

"Well! You see what it gets me."

She smiles wickedly. I didn't know she could do that.

"I'd say it got you a makeout session with the ICU director."

"I thought I would *need* the ICU. Now—you want to stop flirting and give me a little backstory?"

She downs the rest of the glass and pours another. "*You're* driving."

"Story of my life."

"First of all, honeybear, you're dealing with a split personality here. One is me; the other is a repressed Catholic schoolgirl we shall call Mary-Margaret. So. Where to begin? After my brother died, I was going through the well-known steps of grieving—Shock, Anger, Bargaining, et cetera—when I ran into one that Mary-Margaret found highly disagreeable: Intense Horniness."

"Pretty logical," I say. "We react to death by seeking life—through procreation, ergo sex."

She sprouts a death-defying smile. "I love a man who can actually use 'ergo' in a sentence. But you see, I was using you for dual purposes. Primarily, you were my confidante—and a good one, I might add. You have this charming ability to *not* give advice."

"You're welcome."

"On the other hand, I was sorely in need of a fantasy figure for the…relief…of my overcharged libido. Honey, if I had to pay you Screen Actors Guild wages, I'd be bankrupt."

"Point taken."

"And taken and taken. God! I'm a shameless woman. I was wearing my poor dildo to a nub."

The waiter arrives with our burgers. His face is medium-rare.

"Pretending I didn't hear that," he mutters, and steals away.

Pisarro hides her face, trying not to laugh out loud. She eventually recovers, and bites into a fry.

"Why does the waiter always arrive on a word like 'dildo'?"

She samples her burger and washes it down with Dom.

"A rare taste combination. Where was I?"

Michael J. Vaughn   59

"Union wages and dildos."

"Is the plural of 'dildo' oh-ess or oh-ee-ess? Now! Another reason you were such a good therapist, Grinder, was all those tales from your atrocious love life. Which accomplished two things. One, gave me additional visual fuel for my evening sessions. And two, firmly established your utter lack of judgement or ability to maintain a monogamous relationship. Guaranteeing that a wise, professional woman such as myself would never get involved with you.

"Only, it wasn't working. In fact, every time you told me a new Kelly story, it only increased my desire. Then, when you told me the *final* Kelly story—about your golf-course breakup—I realized that you were dangerously available. I began to have all-night wrestling matches with Mary-Margaret. 'But he's married,' she said. 'But he's handsome,' I said. And then I put the little bitch into a half-Nelson.

"By the time of our little picnic, I had soundly defeated her. I invited a known philanderer to a famed makeout spot, wore a very unprofessional bra to work, and accidentally—Oh my!—left a button undone on my blouse.

"But alas, Mary-Margaret was not dead. She was hiding in the bottom of my lunch bag. When you unleashed your Roman hands, she jumped out and pepper-sprayed me with vintage Catholic guilt. The inner conflict demanded escape, so I fled, and covered up my utter hypocrisy with self-righteousness. Later, when I received the pornographic email, Mary-Margaret relished the opportunity to rub your face in it. Dr. Pisarro, on the other hand…wanted to be the girl in the photographs."

I take a slug of Coke and let the bubbles fizz my brain. Yikes! After three months of earnest rehab, I am having schoolboy conflicts of my own. But the schoolboy is getting excited. Pisarro notes my struggle, and sends me a husky laugh.

"I know, Grinder. I seemed like such a naif when you met me. My co-workers call me 'cartoon-girl,' because I look like someone from a Dick and Jane book. Little do they know what evil thoughts lurk behind these den-mother features.

"For instance: that night you first arrived at the ER. Whenever I walked away from your bed, I could feel that one good eye taking measurements of my ass. And yes, a smart woman knows her best anatomical features, and uses them accordingly. I began to leave things at your bedside so I could come back for them and walk slowly away. The best was when your awful porn-star wife was pleading for forgiveness."

The waiter returns, and asks how we're doing.

"Great," I say. "Do you make champagne milkshakes?"

He laughs, relieved that we're not discussing accessories.

"We haven't quite taken the Bubbly Burger that far."

"How 'bout an apple pie, a la mode. Dr. Pisarro?"

"I'll have the same."

Pisarro refills her glass, then sets her lips into a straight line, ready to strategize.

"The carbon-dating girl?" she asks.

"Gone. Apparently a one-time prank."

"No other current hanky-panky?"

"Nada."

"Bueno." She tents her fingers like a judge considering a sentence. "I like to run things, Grinder. That's why I'm running the ICU. So here's the plan. Find a full evening when you can get away. No quickies—I'm willing to wait. Also, I understand you'll have to work things around your children's schedules. Your devotion to them is one of the things that turns me on about you. Send me an email with the time and date of our rendezvous, and I will send your instructions. I've got a long list of plans for you, Mister. And Grinder?"

"Yes, ma'am?"

"The occasional maintenance boink with the wife, I understand. But no one else. Mary-Margaret can only stretch her mores so far. Understood?"

"Yes."

"Good. I'll make you happy, Grinder."

"I get the feeling you will."

An ambulance races down the street, siren blaring. The waiter brings our pies, steaming chunks of apple, vanilla melting down the sides.

CHAPTER 14

My love life depends entirely on my in-laws. Latching onto the musical instruction bandwagon, Grandma Darlene decides to take Laura and her brother to the San Francisco Symphony (the program features a cello concerto). Grandpa Richard tacks on a Sunday tour of Alcatraz, which means a hotel stay Saturday night. The only remaining obstacle is Jessie.

It's Wednesday night. We're washing the dishes. Through everything, this is the ritual that remains. But I'm nervous. It's been a long time since I wanted something this badly. The words are running through my head: *Jess, would you mind if I went bowling Saturday with Marty? He's been pretty down after his divorce and...*

"...I should just spend the night."

"Beg pardon?" I say.

Jessie looks at me with a touch of anxiety, as if she's been caught at something. She repeats her request.

"Helen? Saturday night? She's been awfully down since her Mom died, and I thought a night of chick-flicks would be just the thing. And, since it's all the way in Hollister, I was figuring I should just spend the night."

I'm sure I'm looking overloaded, trying to keep all the expression from my face, but I do manage a half-smile.

"Sure."

She leaves me to dry the silverware, walking away with a lift in her step. This has to be the longest relationship Damon has ever managed.

Pisarro's getting cryptic on me. Her email reads, *Map to my condo follows. 7 p.m. Walk right in (don't knock). Report to the kitchen for instructions.*

62   Double Blind

It's a new-looking building, three blocks uphill from the main strip of San Carlos. The layout's a little wacky. From the front gate, I have to walk downstairs, then take an elevator three stories back up. I'm wandering the walkway, trying to figure out the numbering system, when the next door takes an irrational leap to Pisarro's address.

I do what I'm told and barge right in, a clean entryway of large white tiles and black grouting. The tiles continue leftward into the kitchen, a modern confabulation of blondewood cabinets and gunmetal appliances. At the right is a tiled counter separating kitchen and dining room; this is where I find my instructions, written on the back of a postcard from New Orleans.

Drink a half cup of coffee (warming on coffeemaker behind you). I want your nerve endings open. Report to mantelpiece for further instructions.

I take my java to the living room, divided from the dining room by a stand-alone fireplace. Note number two is on the back of a postcard from Milan, taped to a long, barbecue-style lighter. I sit on the couch before a smoked-glass coffee table (balanced on the back of a bronze female nude) and read the following:

Light the Duraflames in the fireplace. Find the CD player and press play. Adjourn to my balcony, enjoy the view, then enter the door to the right. Proceed to the number one. Do not remove your clothes until you see red. Do not speak.

The Duraflames start up easily. The CD player produces Pavarotti. I carry my coffee to the balcony, which provides a stunning view: the downtown strip, the train station, the downbending arch of the San Mateo Bridge, the East Bay a band of rhinestones shimmering in the cold. I finish my coffee, Pavarotti telling his poet's life to Mimi on the garret floor. I toy with the idea of stopping right here. My destiny lies on the far side of this door; how deliciously tantalizing to leave it unopened, to leave it perfect. I'm fooling no one. I turn the knob; I walk in.

I'm expecting candlelight; I get a lamp, casting the room in sepia. On a large bed, over a spread of gold and copper, lies a black form. The head-piece is a kind of mesh, allowing breath, but the rest is thicker. I sit on the edge of the bed and find that the bodysuit is spotted by numbered patches. I touch the fabric and find that it's velvet.

"We-ell…"

"Sh!" A single, harsh spurt. She's serious. I raise an apologetic hand, and proceed to number one.

It's a six-inch square over her stomach, held at each corner by a knot of string. I pull them loose and lift the fabric to reveal a field of light olive skin, marked by a tangle of cubic snakes. A crossword! I notice a clear filament, tied to one corner of the opening, trailing all the way off the bed. When I pull it, a black pen peeks over the bedspread and crawls my way. It's a permanent marker—evidently, Dr. Pisarro wants this memento to last.

But what of clues? I search the opening for more filaments, then I notice the patch of fabric, its inner skin tattooed with words:

1. *Pepper* _____

2. *Spanish explorer*

3. *Prurient literature*

4. *Cupid's weapon*

5. *Dependable*

6. *Nibble*

7. *Painting*

I fill in *Grinder, Pisarro, erotica, arrow, reliable, bite* and *art,* holding steady on my quivering canvas as she fights the tickles. I blow my letters dry and proceed to number two.

Number two is a half-sock on her left foot. I pull it off to liberate five pedicured tootsies and a slip of paper reading *Dresser*. Upon said dresser I find five colors of nail polish, and set carefully to my work. After ten minutes, Pisarro's piggies are silver, bronze, emerald, hot pink and metallic blue—a strange array if ever I saw one. I blow them dry and run a finger down the middle of her sole. She squirms in protest.

I locate number three on her right forearm, tugging a Velcro patch to reveal a strip of skin, one inch by three, the mound of the flexor muscles descending toward the elbow. No instructions. Being a student of patterns, however, I find a rectangle of paper Scotch-taped to the inside of the patch. But not just paper—sandpaper. Scrawled across the back are the words *Draw blood.*

Game or no game, I'm going to need some confirmation. Then I feel Pisarro's left hand, patting my shoulder, and I know exactly what she wants. Playing soccer, I would sometimes dive across bare soil, and small rocks would tear at my skin. Days later, I would run my hand over the ant-size scabs, and feel an odd tingle of pleasure.

64   Double Blind

I begin slowly, not wanting to go any deeper than necessary. The paper draws white scratch-lines, blushes of pink, then beads of red as the sand breaks through. I wipe my thumb across the blood and lick it off. Pisarro shivers. I blow my work dry, and move on.

Number four is a prize, and Pisarro has treated it accordingly. The circle of felt over her left breast is secured by four loops, threaded through eyelets on the surrounding fabric and held in place by tiny combination locks. The back of each lock confesses its numbers on a strip of white tape, but still it's five minutes before I can unwrap my present, the lovely mound and tan areola that triggered my lunacy four months ago.

So close to the promised land, I am not about to break a rule, so I check the inside of the patch to find the word *Nightstand*. Upon said nightstand, I find a spatula and a small gift-wrapped canister. I open the lid, dip my finger into its creamy white contents and lick off a dollop of vanilla frosting.

Five minutes later, I have completed the finest birthday cake in my 42 years, hiding the final sliver of flesh with a painterly stroke. I see no reason to forgo my pleasure any longer, so I lower my mouth with the intent of cleaning every inch.

I am taking my time, paying extra gratuities to Pisarro's eraser-tip nipple, when her stoicism begins to burst. She squirms against me and opens her legs to reveal the number five. I tear away the Velcroed patch to unveil a carefully shaved arrow of pubic hair, aimed at Pisarro's butterfly-wing labia, beaded with moisture. By this time she is bucking, and I am desperate for instructions. The inside of the patch reads *Shoebox, foot of bed*, and I'm there in a flash. The box contains several phalluses and a bottle of massage oil.

Pisarro isn't going to make it. I start with the handle of a paintbrush, then a tapered candle, going slow, trying to back her off. Next is a peeled carrot, then a zucchini. A dildo of clear plastic. She waves her arms in the air like a gospel singer. I insert the anatomically detailed vibrating penis and her breath turns into bird-like shrieks. She explodes. I hold her torso, watching her pelvis as it describes arcs in the air.

I slide next to her and hold on to her breast as she comes back down. I've known all along that number six resides over Pisarro's mouth. I take off the patch, and receive my invitation with a delighted shiver. I back off the bed and shuck my pants, cup my hand beneath the black, faceless head and lower my cock to Pisarro's red lips.

After three times, I'm feeling like a college kid, enjoying Pisarro's body as a whole, as we curl together before the dying Duraflames.

"The library."

"Ye-es?" she says. She nudges her butt into my groin.

"Got erections there all the time in high school. All that beautiful forced silence. That's what I was thinking tonight when you shushed me, like some dominatrix librarian. Man! I could smell the card catalog."

"You must have been a fun study partner." She pulls my hand to her breast; I see the scratches on her forearm, already clotting. "I didn't really think I could pull this off," she says. "But how often do you get the chance to make a first time so memorable?"

I stretch upward to Pisarro's ear and whisper. "You're an amazing creation."

"Thank you," she replies. "And Mr. Grinder has earned his name."

"So long, Mary-Margaret."

"Good-bye."

CHAPTER 15

I am too attached to logic and the nature of kinetics to have this wish, but I do: *Stop right now. Freeze.*

Because life is perfect. For the price of a few spare hours—mere cracks in the sidewalk of my week—I have achieved a strolling paradise. We meet every day for lunch. No need to hide—we are well known as friends. If we feel the need to crank up the touchy-feely, we head for a restaurant with a dark booth.

In a way, however, the constant restraint is pleasing. I have learned the joy of discipline, of saving up my pennies. Every once in a while, the in-laws steal my children, Jessie makes her expected excuses, and I receive an entire evening of Pisarro.

You wouldn't guess this from our first encounter, but the sex is not all that wild. She does throw curveballs—body paints, Halloween costumes out of season ("Naughty Cop!®")—but no major productions. Most of the time, it's comfortable, and direct. You might even call it lovemaking. The first time *that* word popped into my head, I was microwaving popcorn in the break room. I neglected to listen for the three-second gap between pops, and burned my kernels to a charcoal crisp. (My co-workers spent the afternoon anonymously cursing me for the smell.) This is the first time in years that I have had sex with a person and not a fantasy figure. Not since Nancy.

Let me tell you about Pisarro. Pisarro uses soap made from melon and cucumber. She wears a silver band on her right ring finger that her father gave her the year before he died. Her eyelashes are so long that she never wears mascara (but she's constantly tugging them, to keep them out of her eyes). She hates country music with a passion. She cries at the sight of snapdragons, but can't say why.

Today we're touchy-feely at the Café Borrone in Menlo Park. The place is too well lit, but we're camped in a far corner near the restrooms. I'm sipping at a frosted mocha, spiked with bits of coffee bean. It's a beautiful drink.

"I'm stunned," says Pisarro. "I was expecting politics. My boss *told* me there would be politics. Two of the people on my staff applied for—and did not get—my job. Two months, no politics. They follow my every bidding, like a staff of Stepford wives."

"No surprise there. It's the natural reaction to your sparkling personality and radiating competence."

Little half-moons of light glimmer at the corners of her eyes. (How does she do that?)

"How sweet! You memorized the script I sent you this morning." She rubs a hand around my thigh, extending a finger to tickle my scrotum. "I don't mean to push, Hopkins, but when do we get to play again?"

I flash her a grin filled with secret knowledge.

"Ooh!" she says. "Is this good news?"

"It is. They're sending me to Northwestern for a week to set up a new lab. I leave in three weeks. I was hoping you could get some time off and…"

"Yes!" She leans across the table to give me an involved kiss. I hear my mother-in-law ordering a panini sandwich. The counter is fifteen feet away. I place a hand on Pisarro's shoulder, pull smoothly away and spin for the restroom door.

I'm in the hallway. The men's room is occupied. Shit! I duck into the women's. I am vaguely disappointed. Where are the floral-scented tissues? The basket of chocolate mints? I check the mirror, rub a spot of lipstick from my mouth, and look around for something to write on.

A minute later, I'm ready to make my break. I crack open the door. There's Darlene.

"Hopkins!" She smiles, then slowly cogitates my crime. "Hopkins!" she scolds.

"It's a compulsion," I say. "I sneak into women's rooms and leave the seat up."

Darlene emits a squeaky laugh. "Hopkins! You're such a cut-up. Give your mum-in-law a hug."

That's how it works with Mother Zwei. One must first wait for an invitation. Only then should one slide in for a light, respectful embrace.

"Are you here on your lunch?" she asks.

"Yes. I love the paninis here."

"No! I just ordered one. Can you stay and talk? I'm here with my old pal Maggie, and I'm sure she'd love to meet you."

I extract my pocketwatch. "Oh! You know, I really can't. I'm late for a meeting. Nice running into you, though."

She dons her phoniest smile. "Can't stand in the way of cancer research. Say hello to my daughter and lovely grandchildren."

"I will. Ta!"

"Ta!" she says, and heads into the restroom.

I swing through the door at a brisk pace, dropping a note as I pass Pisarro's table. Ten minutes later, I'm a block away at a used bookstore, thumbing through a medical dictionary. Pisarro peers around the bookshelf.

"Well! That was fun. Friend of yours?"

"Mother-in-law."

"Holy Shee-boygan."

"Yeh."

She holds up a tampon, still in its wrapper. "Nice note."

"They were out of paper towels. Good thing I had quarters."

"I'll say. I'll trade you for this." She hands me a to-go cup, filled with the remains of my frosted mocha.

"Jesus! Are you really this good?"

She flashes a cocksure smile. "I'm even better."

CHAPTER 16

I derive an insane amount of pleasure from the people movers at San Francisco International. Walk a normal pace and you're covering ground like Superman, several feet at a stride. It's a downright bummer when you reach the end and have to return to your earthly creep.

I tug my suitcase into long-term parking, where I pay ridiculous rates for the luxury of familiarity: preset radio buttons, the rear-view just so, the shift worn smooth at the palm of my hand.

I have had my little joke on California, which suffered a weeklong storm while I walked around in mid-70s Chicago sunshine. Ha! I am so god-like that I control the weather.

Sorry. I'm giddy on snapshots. We share an armchair in the hotel lounge, watching football as Pisarro explains the imminent death of the West Coast Offense. We climb the steps at the Art Institute, past Rodin's *Adam* into a room of ice-cream Renoirs, my fingers laced into hers. We slip under the space-age latticework of Millennium Park, security guards noodling around the broad stage, setting up for a concert. Pisarro beckons me to the shag lawn, then kneels behind me to rub my shoulders.

"What are we going to do with each other?"

"We've already done a lot," I tease.

She slaps the top of my head. "You know what I mean."

"Yes, I do. And you know that I intend to keep my children."

"I know the price of the ride, honey. A ride that I *so* enjoy. I'm just fighting off the Gimme More Syndrome."

"Mary-Margaret?"

"The little bitch has been looking at bridal magazines."

70   Double Blind

"It's not forever," I say. "Let me get them through high school."

"You're a good man, Grinder. Now, lie down on your back."

I'm looking skyward at a speaker, dangling from the organic-looking metallic beams like a fruit on a speaker-tree. The Sears Tower looms to my right, fuzzy in the sunlight. Pisarro straddles me and leans forward till her face is inches away.

"I love you, Grinder. I love you a ridiculous amount. Don't answer. Just nod your head. Good boy."

Her eyes get closer. Her eyes disappear. The Sears Tower disappears.

Pulling into my driveway. I am missing another girl. And a boy. But the house is empty and silent. A wind chime tinkles in the backyard.

"Laura? Marcus?" I turn and start for the master bedroom. "Jessie?"

Jessie is flat on the bed, fully clothed, whimpering into her pillow. I touch her on the shoulder. She turns with red eyes, scrambles to the edge and plants her face in my sweater.

"Hopkins."

She says it as if she's reminding herself of my name.

"Take me…Montalvo."

I'm driving my wife to Montalvo so she can tell me where my kids are. She's eerily quiet, staring out the window as we motor the uphills of Saratoga.

Montalvo is an old mansion, built in 1912 by a San Francisco mayor. Jessie and I came here on our first date, a jazz concert in the back garden. We had our first kiss on the front terrace, next to the balustrade railings, under garlands of white wisteria. No wonder she loved me.

The blossoms are gone, given way to a summer-green blanket of leaves and pods. Jessie stops at the railing, a genuflection of memory, and continues down the steps to the sprawling front lawn. At the bottom is a grassy mound that turns out to be hollow, a piece of art-installation built from sod.

Jessie finds an arched entry and ducks inside, then heads for the center, where the artist has cut a circle into the domed ceiling. The stark light turns her hair brilliant, angelic. She takes a long breath and turns to face me.

"Hold back on anger, Hopkins. This is…complicated. First thing: the kids are fine. They're with Mom and Dad. Where do I start?"

She paces away, slapping a hand against her thigh.

"About a month after I started sleeping with Damon…" She pauses to check me with a look. "He offered me a chance to make some money. Anybody who knows me would guess that I slapped him and left. I didn't. I said yes, and I appeared on a porn site."

"Horny Housewives," I say.

"So you knew. Okay. I wasn't sure." She looks at the dirt floor. "I was kind of…a hit. Damon says I have this quality of looking like precisely the last person in the world who would be fucking on a website. Suburban Ice Queen."

She laughs to herself.

"I really liked it, Hopkins. But it wasn't the sex, and not the money—certainly not Damon. It was power. My body was triggering the desires of strange men. Thousands of men going erect, masturbating, coming at the sight of my body.

"I haven't had power in a long time. Not since I married you. You didn't love me, but you married me anyway. And we had children. You love the children, but you don't love me. Why is that, Hopkins? *I* gave birth to them."

She stares at the entryway, trying to regain her story.

"You remember…You remember this October? When I was so well behaved? It wasn't an act. I was so incredibly comfortable in my own skin. We were *even*, Hop. I had my little secret, and…we were even. Until Damon let slip that you had set up the whole thing."

She fans her fingers, like a magician disappearing a quarter.

"All my power…"

"I didn't know about the website," I say. "I thought he was just going to sleep with you, and…it's weird, I know, but I just wanted you to be happy."

She levels a stare.

"You wanted me out of the way. You wanted me to stop being so much trouble."

I stare right back.

"I wanted my children to stop being afraid of you. I wanted you not to attack me with sharp objects."

She takes it, considers it, and drops it.

"Okay. Okay. But consider my situation. Once more, *you're* the instigator. *You're* the one with the power. I couldn't even cheat on you…without *you* arranging it. Jesus!"

She runs a hand along the dirt ceiling.

"So I decided, if I couldn't bring myself up, I would bring *you* down. I began by screwing a large black man. Horace. You know him?"

"I'm familiar with his work."

She laughs, then returns to the circle of light and crosses her arms.

72   Double Blind

"You remember the lemonade? Daffy Jessie and her oversexed lemon tree?"

"Sure."

"You remember how they made you feel?"

I think back to my strange longings, the week I attacked Pisarro. They stopped every evening, when I came home. I guess I attributed it to the presence of my children.

"A tiny, tiny bit of vodka," she says. "Not enough for you to notice. Just enough to tap into that lovely family chemistry, and set you back on your heels. And then..."

I can hear the name before she says it.

"Nefertiti."

This one gets me. "You!? You did that? Are you fucking crazy?"

"Yes. I was. But I knew what I was doing. Neffie's harmless. She's lined up for Damon's 'barely legal' site—as soon as she turns eighteen. Meanwhile, she's happy to scare the shit out of horny old men."

"And the Ecstasy?"

"I checked on the drug policies at the lab. I knew you'd get off easy. And I was making enough money to cover us if anything happened. Frankly, I didn't mind serving you up a little humility, honey. And I also didn't mind playing you like a Wurlitzer. Might give you an idea how it feels on *this* side."

The fire goes out of her eyes; she puts a hand on my shoulder. I'd forgotten the color of those eyes: a pale blue that can be downright disconcerting.

"You weren't the only one to be humbled," she says. "I realized halfway through that shoot with Horace that I'd gone too far. It might be hard to understand, but before, when it was just me and Damon and the camera guy, it seemed...friendly. All of a sudden, I'm having sex with this man I just met. It was too much. I told Damon to pull all my stuff from the site. Legally speaking, he didn't have to—but he did, because he likes me. You run into ethical people in the weirdest places.

"Weren't we okay for a while, Hopkins? You were so well behaved. Christmas was beautiful. And those Little League games. It almost felt like we were dating again. I guess I thought I had a chance."

The last words come in a rush, and she chokes up. She turns away and walks into the darkness.

"A couple...a couple weeks ago, my mother saw you with the doctor. She took great pleasure in reporting it back to me. She's such a miserable old bitch. Half of my problem is trying to live her life instead of my own. All those phony ideas of perfection. Well, that tore it. I'd been keeping something special in my back pocket.

"Jeri's a friend of Mom's from Junior League—but around my age. High-tech perfect blonde yuppie lady. Stanford MBA. And a nasty little bisexual streak. Nowhere to let it out, so she would stay late at work and surf the porn sites. Imagine her surprise when she happened on Darlene Zwei's daughter! She got my email address from Mom, told me how much she admired me, how courageous I was. She decided maybe she needed to do something like that herself—'going public,' having it out, once and for all. Maybe a lesbian scene on 'Horny Housewives.'

"But I wasn't aware that Dad was on to me. I guess he could tolerate adultery, or interracial adultery—but cunnilingus with a family friend…"

She pins me with a look.

"They took the kids to Tahoe. They're talking with lawyers."

Her meaning sinks in, and I need escape. I head back outside and sit with my back to the turf wall. Jessie comes out and slides down next to me. My mind is drifting; I'm in the mood to let it.

"Cantinflas."

Jessie blinks. "Oh. Cantinflas. Well, you know the setup. They pretend to pick us up and boink us in front of hidden cameras. It's all bullshit, of course. Damon's got more lawyers than Donald Trump. I signed a shitload of releases, and believe it or not, one of them allows his graphics guy to Photoshop a specific tattoo onto my body. It's designed as a public indication of my willingness to participate in 'said recorded activities.'"

I want to laugh, but my triggers are off, and I find myself crying.

"Jesus, Jess. Are we gonna lose our kids?"

Jessie lays her head on the grass wall and closes her eyes.

"I don't know, Hop. I don't know."

CHAPTER 17

In a 1989 study, the Kinsey Institute conducted a survey of 1,974 American adults. Here's where those adults got their sexual information growing up: friend (42%), mother (29%), books (22%), boyfriend or girlfriend (17%), sex education (14%), magazines (13%)—and in seventh place, at 12%, fathers. Thirty-seven percent of married men said they'd had affairs, 29 percent of married women.

And this: only twenty percent of divorces were caused by infidelity or adultery. "Disagreements about money, family and personal goals, how to spend nonwork hours, and other nonsexual conflicts are the most commonly stated causes of divorce."

I'm reduced to renting a car and spying on my own children. The drive is beautiful, ridges of granite knife-sharp against the blue. I feel guilty, enjoying it so much, but perhaps I am due. I reach the lake, head eastward past summering ski runs, then back uphill toward the sprawling Zwei cabin. (Funny thing about that word; in ski country, even a five-bedroom house is a "cabin.")

I edge the nose of my temporary compact around the corner, and take note of the silver SUV in the driveway. It's difficult to stop, so close to my semi-abducted children, but the reasoning scientist pops up once again to have his way with me. *Assuming your in-laws have assembled a ruse to shelter Laura and Marcus from the truth,* he says, *your sudden appearance would do nothing but harm.*

I swing a yooey and settle into a turnout a block away. My only chance is to speak to Richard alone, so I'm betting he'll take off on an errand. Then I'll tail him to some grocery store and reveal my presence. I have the Sunday *Chroni-*

cle, a thermos of coffee and a sack lunch to see me through. And yes, I realize I'm on a stakeout.

An hour goes by. I'm down to the last letter in the crossword when a wall of silver flashes by. In the receding squares of window I pick out Darlene's bundled hair, plus enough backseat limbs to indicate one Laura, one Marcus. I am considering this sudden turnabout—dast I knock at the door?—when a loud rap defibrillates my heart. It's Richard, peering in at the passenger-side window. I fumble for the button and roll it down. He looks amused, but not necessarily happy.

"I sent them off for pizza," he says. "One of those places with Skee Ball and Wack-A-Mole and such. Come on up to the house."

"How'd you know I was here?"

"I've had this cabin thirty years. I know a strange car when I see one. Besides, I was expecting you."

I look at him over the car roof. "Why?"

"Because we're the men," he says. "And once the shitpile gets this high, it's up to us to shovel it."

He heads up the hill. I follow, feeling like a schoolkid headed for the principal's office.

The Zwei cabin sits atop a ridge, affording a view that hits you like icewater to the chest. The effect is magnified by the living room window, which is basically a wall of glass. I sit on the monster leather couch so I can take it in. Richard hands me a root beer—made by a microbrewery in Sacramento. He keeps them on hand just for me, just so the alcoholic can feel more at home. He settles into an armchair with a bottle of beer.

"You'd think I'd get tired of this vista. I never do." He takes a swallow, lets out a cleansing sigh, then begins his story. This is every bit the closing argument.

"When Jessie was four, she arranged a strip show in the tool shed. Had a curtain made out of old sheets, a couple of flashlight spotlights, and pasties made out of Band-Aids and pipe cleaners. I didn't find out till years later, when a friend of hers was telling old tales at a Christmas party. Apparently, the show was broken up by the ice cream man—the power of the Fudgesicle, at that age, still outranking that of the naked ta-ta.

"In junior high, when the hormones hit, I knew we had trouble on our hands. The way the principal told it, Jessie would chase some boy around the schoolyard, knock him down, and demand to see his wee-wee.

"Her mother tried the zero-tolerance game, but I could see where that was going, and I wasn't ready to be a grandfather. When Jessie was fourteen, I sat her down and told her everything—and I mean to say Tab A, Slot B *everything*. Then I handed her a jumbo box of condoms, and told her that any boy who refused to use one was not good enough for her. *Then*, I took out a Polish kielbasa and demonstrated the application of said condoms."

Despite the seriousness of the situation, I find myself laughing.

"Yes. It is funny," he says. "But it *was* necessary. Jessie had boyfriend after boyfriend, but she never got pregnant. Never kept any of those boys very long, either. I think she scared 'em off.

"'Course, when she got to thirty-five and I *still* wasn't a grandfather, I was beginning to think that I had done too good of a job. But then came you, our Prince Charming. Still, I worried about Jessie's previous…habits, and I could see the effects of her battling them off. The more she suppressed her sexuality, the more she also squashed her sense of humor. She used to have one, you know."

I think about our first few dates, filled with laughter. "Yeah."

"She became a bitch, just like her mother, with one important difference. Darlene's a bitch to everyone else, but not to me—and in the bedroom, she is the most generous of women. I don't need details, Hop, but how were things for you and Jessie, say, a year ago?"

"Pretty dry."

"That was my guess. It seemed to me that Jessie was overcompensating, and I'll tell ya, it's like pulling back a rock on a giant slingshot. Sooner or later, that sucker's gonna fly, and it's going to do some damage. When Jessie showed up on that porn site…"

"About that porn site," I say. "I need to tell you something. After the eye incident, I saw the need to calm Jessie down, or at least distract her. So I arranged for a friend of a friend to…have a go at her. As it turns out, he's also the guy who runs 'Horny Housewives.'"

"I see." Richard rubs his mustache. "But she did appear on the site voluntarily."

"As it turns out, yes."

"Okay. If it makes you feel better, we'll assign twenty percent of the blame to you. But blame is not the point. This is a matter of true natures—and Jessie is still the four-year-old in the strip show. You're the geneticist, you know how this works. The core self does not change all that much."

"No. It doesn't."

"Jessie did such a good job of hiding her inclinations, you couldn't have known that you were throwing gasoline on a fire."

"Richard! I'm not one of your clients, so stop building a case for me. I have contributed my fair share of nastiness to this situation. And I have never loved your daughter—not when I married her, not when we had Marcus, or Laura. Never. Don't you think there's a special level of hell reserved for *that* kind of selfishness?"

Richard seems to tire of the argument, and paces toward the window to retrack his thoughts.

"Let's cut to the chase, Hopkins. As you have probably figured out, I have no legal right to take your children. Appearing on porn sites is not against the law. But I do have a say over Jessie's inheritance, and your children's trust funds. And I'm also betting on the respect that *you* hold for *me*. A respect that I like to think I have earned. So here's the brass tacks: I want you to divorce my daughter."

I jump up from the couch. "No! My children will *not* grow up in a broken home."

Richard studies my reaction. "Okay, Hop. Now I *will* build a case for you. This is my courtroom, and you will answer me directly—no psychobabble, no emotional nonsense. First: Why, precisely, do you not want your kids to grow up in a broken home?"

"Because *I* did! And it sucks! It's awful."

"Okay," he says. "Now. Think like a scientist, Hopkins. What kind of evidence is your specific childhood?"

My thoughts are firing in all directions. But I am reined in by Richard's instructions, and I know the answer.

"Anecdotal."

"And tell me, Mr. Grinder. What is the value of anecdotal evidence, under scientific standards?"

"Worthless. Its only value is to illustrate the results of an expansive, double-blind study."

I sit back on the couch, soundly defeated. Richard comes over and puts a hand on my shoulder.

"Keeping a family together is the noblest pursuit I can think of, Hop. But your wife is screwing strange men on a public website. The end no longer justifies the means. I won't sit here, as a grandfather, and allow it to continue."

I'm feeling penned-in, so I head for the balcony, where the fresh air resuscitates me. Richard arrives a minute later and hands me a fresh root beer.

"I'm sorry we had to go to such…extremes to get your attention. But I made a promise to look out for your children. I didn't say you'd always agree with me about it. And don't worry—I'm not cutting Jessie loose. I'll do whatever I can to help her out."

I take a long swig on my root beer.

"You're the closest thing to a father I've ever had, Richard."

"I'm honored." He leans against the railing and joins me in scanning the lake. "'Course, now I get to explain to my wife how I just talked you into divorcing my daughter."

"First thing," I say. "Remove all sharp objects from the kitchen."

Finally, we get to laugh.

When I arrive home, late that night, I do something very unusual: I make love to my wife. Our sex is slow and careful—because we know it's our last. Afterward, Jessie sits on the edge of the bed, gazing into a mirror over the dresser.

"So what's the decision?"

"He wants us to get a divorce."

"Nice of *him* to decide that."

"I want it, too."

She turns to look at me.

"You…do?"

I kneel behind her and comb my hands through her hair. I used to do this when we first met.

"We need to stop the power games, Jessie. And we need to stop being other people."

"But this *is* me!"

"I know. That's exactly what I mean. You're a wild, sexual being, and you've been holding it in for too long. I, meanwhile, who want nothing more than a happy, stable family life, have been pursuing it by screwing sixteen-year-olds."

"And doctors."

"And doctors." (I have considered 'fessing up about Kelly, as well, but it serves no purpose.) "Brass tacks, honey? This carefully constructed façade is going to crumble, one way or the other. Rather than letting it crush our kids underneath, why don't you and I take it apart, piece by piece?"

"Will I get to see them?"

"Yes. But your father is holding some rather important cards, so…"

"God damn him!" She stands and slams the wall with the palm of her hand.

"Jess. Look at it from your father's point of view. From your father's *generation*. All things considered, the man is a marvel of understanding."

"He told you the stories, didn't he?"

"Yes."

She leans her head against the wall and starts to cry.

I stand and take my wife in my arms. "You can't have everything, sweet Jessie. But maybe you can have a little of each. Okay?"

"Okay."

CHAPTER 18

If not for my best friend, Greg Love, I might not have survived my childhood. Greg's family seemed to understand the situation with my mother, and afforded me stepson status, free to come and go, and to stay for the occasional sleepover.

One Saturday, when I was eight, Mom was having a bad hangover, and naturally blaming everybody else for it, so I walked around the corner and found Greg's family having a garage sale. But Greg was out shopping with his mom, so I busied myself looking through a box of old magazines. Near the bottom, I found a copy of *Scientific American* featuring two shots of a funny-looking fish, turning color from a dull gray to a dazzling red-and-white.

Come mating season, the male three-spined stickleback (*Gasterosteus aculeatus*) builds a nest on the sandy bottom of a freshwater shallow and guards it fiercely. Then he changes to his bright courtship colors and tries to attract females. Once a female lays eggs in his nest, he sweeps in to fertilize them, chases the female away and goes looking for another.

After escorting three to five females through this process, the male's red color darkens, and he grows increasingly hostile to females. He guards the nest from predators, fans water over the eggs to enrich their supply of oxygen, and then watches over the hatchlings for a day, until they're able to fend for themselves.

I gave Greg's father a nickel, took the magazine home and pinned the cover on my wall. When my mother asked me about it, I said, "That's the three-spined stickleback; he's my hero." She assumed I was joking.

Michael J. Vaughn   81

I'm looking through some emails from Chicago when I spy Marty's cowlick, bobbing over the cubicle wall like a single-wing blackbird. The rest of him appears at the opening.

"Hopkins! I wanted to congratulate you."

"Hi, Marty. From what I hear, *you're* the one who gets congratulated. When do you leave for Chi-town?"

He looks puzzled. "Shy Town?"

"Man! We gotta get you lingo'd up. The Windy City. City of Broad Shoulders. That Toddlin' Town. Are you aware that Sinatra had *two* hit songs about Chicago?"

He cocks his head like a curious puppy. "Sinatra?"

"Oh! Marty!" I hide my face in my hands—but in truth, I love Marty's cultural gaps. They illustrate all the assumptions that Americans make about being the center of the world. Despite my joshing, Marty's expression turns serious.

"Do you think, Hopkins, that I will make a good leader?"

I give this a thorough consideration. Marty is intensely skeptical, and will not fall for the usual platitudes.

"Yes. But you have to find a leadership style that suits your personality. I see you as someone who builds respect in a quiet manner, by conferring with your colleagues before making big decisions, and making sure they know what's expected of them. A democratic leader—a diplomat."

"Thanks," he says. "I'll keep that in mind." He lifts a foot and taps the ground nervously. "I am assuming…from the good news, that the information I had previously…that things have worked out?"

I'm distracted by a photo on my desk, Laura beaming from a piano.

"Yes, Marty. It was tricky. But yes, everything worked out. And I appreciate your ability to keep a secret. That's another thing that will serve you well in Chicago."

Marty smiles. "The City of Shy Shoulders?"

"I'm gonna miss you, Marty."

"I will miss you, too. Oh, and we will have a going-away party on Thursday."

"Great! I'll see you then."

Marty's cowlick flies away down the hall, and I return to my email. But then I notice the clock, and grab my jacket.

Times have changed. When I see Pisarro at Café Borrone, I lift her off the ground, right in front of the patio diners. We order a couple of paninis and find a table next to the fountain.

"How's life at the lab?" she asks—but something's up. Her eyes are even larger than usual. One of these days, she's going to stretch those peepers too far and sprain a ligament.

"The lab is fine, oh walking dictionary."

"Pardon?"

"'Cause I can read you like a book. You don't give a rat's ass about the lab."

She grins and reaches into her purse. "I guess I'll just have to show you."

She presents me with a black velvet box, and clicks it open to reveal a large sapphire in a platinum setting.

"Wow!" I take it out and give it a close study. The sunlight comes through from behind, winking in the facets. The color is a bright royal blue, remarkably clear.

"No diamonds? I mean, around the edges?"

"Must I recite the 'diamonds are imperialist bullshit' lecture once more? Sparkly, inflated nothings? Give me *blue*."

I lean over to kiss her. "You are a wonder of style and taste."

"Yes, I am. And thanks for letting me handle this. I realize it goes against the norm."

"Norms are not my interest."

"And for you…" She hands me a second box, containing a platinum band. I slip it on; it's perfect. Were it white gold, it would be exactly the same as my first wedding band. Pisarro gives me a concerned look.

"It's not too soon?"

I take her hand. "It's about fifteen years too late."

She kisses my ring finger. "What about the kids?"

"Won't be easy. It's a fine balance. Don't try to be a mom the moment we get back from the honeymoon. But don't let them play on your guilt, either. They give you any trouble, you send them to Papa."

"Have you been…preparing them?"

"Yes. I talk to them a lot."

"What do you say?"

"I tell them the truth, in the nicest way I can manage."

"Minus the porn site?"

"There's truth, and there's mental abuse."

Michael J. Vaughn   83

Pisarro starts a laugh that gets out of control, elevating to giggles before she squashes them in her hand and stares at the fountain.

"God, Grinder. I'm a giddy schoolgirl. One minute I'm hovering down the sidewalk, the next I'm in a complete panic. It's terrifying! And incredibly exciting."

"We'll be good, Pisarro. Now eat your panini! We have to get back to work."

After work, I head to an industrial park, one of many left vacant by the Silicon Valley cooldown. The parking lot is ghostly empty, but the bordering lawns are still lush and green. I peer into the windows at long fields of cubicles, then cut around the corner of the building to a baseball field, backed up against the high sound-walls of the interstate.

Most of the team is packing up and leaving, but Marcus crouches at third, tackling grounders and making erratic throws to first. The first baseman leaps this way and that, like a man with a butterfly net going after hummingbirds. Marcus's coach, Ed Collitos, stands at the plate, shouting advice.

"You're still thinking, Marcus! You're still aiming. Try it this way: imagine that the ball is covered with a deadly substance. Get rid of that thing as fast as you can, and don't worry if Karl catches it. Okay?"

He hits a slow hopper. Marcus charges it, nabs it with his glove and throws mid-step. The ball short-hops Karl and bounces away.

"Yes!" says Ed.

"That was awful!" Marcus complains.

"Style, not results. Now remember—poisonball!" He smacks a one-hopper. Marcus catches the ball at his knees and fires across the diamond. Karl smacks it into his glove, chest-high.

Ed raises both hands. "Yes! You see? You see how that feels? Remember that feeling. Time to quit—your dad's here."

I arrive at the dugout as Marcus is untying his laces.

"Third base, huh?"

"Yeah. If I learn to throw."

"Last one looked good."

"Hmmph. You missed the other twenty-seven."

I'm not in the mood to press my case, so I try a different tack.

"Third's a lot of fun. Y'gotta learn how to yell, though. When a runner's trying to score from second, you got the best seat in the house, so you have to tell your cutoff man if he's got a chance."

"Geez, I'm not good at yelling."

84   Double Blind

"I know."

"What do I say?"

"Just yell the base. 'Home!' 'Third!' 'Second!'"

He ties up his tennies and zips his bat-bag. "Did you want to be a ballplayer, Dad?"

"Ha! Me and every kid in America."

We start across the field. During the past year, my fatherhood satellite dish has become very finely tuned, and I'm picking up something...fidgety in Marcus's manner. It doesn't come out till we're in the car, waiting to get on the freeway.

"John Wehner's parents got divorced, and his mom moved to Florida. He says he never sees her."

We stop next to a homeless guy with a cardboard sign, all the usual stuff: Vietnam vet, God bless, two hungry children. How soon till we get 'Iraq vet'?"

"You know your mom's staying here, right? And she'll come to your games, and you'll see her all summer?"

He taps his glove against the dash. "Yeah. I know."

I can read his next thought: *You also said, "Till death do us part."* In the stream of failure that is divorce, you spend a lot of time wondering if you should make any promises at all. Why should they believe a single thing you say?

"I guess all I can say, Marcus, is that your mother and I have spent a lot of time planning this out. And your mother and I are still friends."

"Don't say 'your mother.'"

"Pardon?"

"Don't say 'your mother.' And don't freak out—it's not some big symbolic thing. Just call her 'Jessie,' like you would if you were talking to an adult."

I can't help it. The kid makes me smile.

"What?" he says.

"I guess I *am* talking to an adult. And *Jessie's* not going to Florida."

The light turns, and we climb the onramp. Marcus takes off his cap and puts it on inside-out. In baseball parlance, this is what's known as a "rally cap."

"See?" he says. "Was that so hard?"

I manage to prepare a decent dinner (God bless that Hamburger Helper) and am soon embarked on the Get Thee to Bed routine with Laura. This is a steady countdown of alerts—the thirty-minute alert, the ten-minute alert, the I-really-mean-it alert—designed to nudge my darling daughter to the trinity of toilet, toothbrush and bed. I have considered purchasing a cattle prod (but what parent hasn't?).

Before my departure, I stop by to tuck her in. She regards me coolly, like a lawyer sizing up his opponent.

"Dadsalish."

I sit bedside, in an old kitchen chair.

"Lauralish."

"I'd like to ask you some questions."

"Okay. But I'm short on time. Can we make it three questions?"

She smiles. "Like a genie?"

"Exactly. Fire away."

She crosses her arms over the edge of her blanket. "First question: what, exactly, will be my relationship with Pisarro?"

This is a good sign. She's noticed the way that Pisarro and I call each other by our last names, and has adopted it for herself.

"Your father loves Dr. Pisarro very much, and holds a deep admiration for her. If you value your father's judgement—and I suspect you do—you will look for these same fine qualities that he sees in her, and I expect that you will find them."

"Daddy? Why are you talking about yourself like you're not here?"

"Sorry. Daddy's been watching too many sports interviews. Where was I? Oh! Your mother. Your mother will always be your mother. Pisarro will never try to take her place. But, Pisarro is an adult, and during those times when I ask her to look out for you, I will expect you to obey and respect her."

"Okay."

I cross my arms, genie-like. "Next question!"

"Okay. You know how Mom visits us, here at the house?"

"Yes."

"Will you do that when we're staying with Mom?"

"Absolutely. Except for August…"

"When you and Pisarro go to Ireland."

"Exactamundo. Next!"

"Okay." She fiddles with the satin fringe on her blanket. This one's a toughie.

"Lauralish? What did we say about questions?"

"No matter what the question, or how dumb it might seem…"

"Ask it!" I finish.

"Okay. Was it…me?"

86   Double Blind

I expect more, but it's not coming. "Was it you…what?"

"Did I do something to break up you and Mom?"

Shew. I've been expecting this one. But how much of it do you truly answer? The stock reply is, *It's not about you, honey.* But a Daughter of Grinder deserves something more substantial.

"Your mother and I have had problems for a lot of years, honey. We tried to work those problems out, and stay together, because we love you and Marcus very much, and we thought staying together was what would be best for you. After a while, though, we realized that our problems were too big—that we were spending all of our time on our problems instead of on raising you. So we decided…it was time for a change.

"So no, honey. It's not something that you did. But we are always thinking of what's best for you, and we always will. Okay?"

"I still wish you were together."

I grip her shoulder and kiss her on the cheek. "I know, honey. You gonna sleep now?"

"Mmmaybe."

"Maybe my rear end! Let's hear some Z's!"

She closes her eyes and lets out a snore loud enough for a 300-pound man.

"That's what I like to hear. Marcus is in charge till I get back, okay?"

She opens one eye. "Do I have to obey and respect him?"

"Well. At least obey."

She snickers as I switch off the light.

"Good night, Lauralish."

"'Night, Popsalish."

It's a long trip—all the way to I-5, north of Stockton. Just when you think you're in bumfuck nowhere, a red sign sprouts from the fields: *ADULT SHOPPE, Open 24 Hours.* The old-fashioned spelling cracks me up. It's a short turn off the freeway, a sharp right off the farm road and I'm pulling into the parking lot, headlights glaring back in the double glass doors.

I enter to the jangle of bells and miles of shelving: DVDs, videos, magazines, lubes, whips, handcuffs, artificial vaginas, cheerleader outfits and Nefertiti.

"Hi! Welcome to Jessie's House of Orgasms. Hopkins."

I point a playful finger. "You naughty girl!"

"Yeah." She's wearing a low-cut Indian maiden vest with fringes. "Sorry 'bout that. I'm hoping I can…make amends?"

"Why, if I wasn't a married and simultaneously engaged man…"

Michael J. Vaughn 87

Jessie makes her appearance through a curtain of hanging beads.

"Actually, she's already making amends. Neffie's running the store while I take care of *your* children. Hi Jasper!"

A burly trucker jangles in, wearing an old cowboy hat of brown suede.

"Hi Jess. Got the new *Naughty Neighbors*?"

"Yep. You know where they are. Geez, Jasper. Maybe you should just subscribe."

"And leave a paper trail for the matrimonial detective agency? I don't think so. That's the beauty of truckin', honey. Gives a man some time away to indulge his crasser instincts. During my stints at home, I am the most perfectly behaved husband in the world."

Jasper tips his cap, and proceeds to the magazine aisle.

Jessie smiles, and turns back to me.

"Well. There's your marketing report. That's why we're way the heck out here. Truckers are the *best* customers. Half the time, they're just happy to get off the road for a minute."

"I'll relay that to your silent partner."

In a strictly business sense, I'm sure Richard would be pleased. A quick scan reveals a dozen customers, including a couple college-age girls giggling at the inflatable hermaphrodites.

"We're a ways from making back our initial investment," says Jessie. "But we're getting there much faster than I expected."

"That's great." I use my next question as an excuse to look back at Neffie—but of course I'm running more private video than Aisle D. "Any place we can talk alone?"

"Sure. Follow me."

She walks me back through the beads into Jessie's Hall of Dildos, which is exactly like a porcupine turned inside-out.

"I wanted to give each its own special 'product placement,'" says Jessie. "See that one in the bullseye? Go ahead—give it a yank."

"Eew! Do I have to?"

She dresses me down with a look. "Like you haven't yanked your own a gazillion times."

"Oh fine."

The bullseye penis triggers a hundred luminescent cousins, dangling from the ceiling in rainbow colors.

"My God!" I exclaim. "It's a veritable dickstorm!"

"Yeah," Jessie laughs. "And that one in the bullseye is a life-cast of Damon."

"Double-eew! Get me outta here."

She lets out that witchy cackle that I still haven't gotten used to and opens a door to the back lot. Across the gravel spread is a warehouse-looking building with metal walls. We enter through a small door, into an office. Except for a dozen copies of *Adult Video News* and a wind-up breast on the desk, it's pretty normal-looking. I notice a framed picture next to her computer, Laura and Marcus at Christmas, adorning each other's faces with bows and ribbons. Jessie takes great pleasure in perching on her large leather desk chair.

"Please. Take a seat on my...casting couch."

"I've heard about you producers—but I'm *not* that kind of guy."

"According to Neffie, you're *exactly* that kind of guy."

"Okay, you got me." Trying to get into the spirit of things, I pick up a copy of *Pleasant Plumpers*. "So. Did you get the papers?"

"Sent them in yesterday. We'll soon be official."

"You're all set for the summer?"

"Yes. I got this wonderful place in Mountain View. Two blocks from downtown, but really quiet. Right across from the library."

I find a perky blonde pudge with marvelous round ass-cheeks. "No...business while you're there?"

"As agreed. Neffie is under strict orders to deny my existence. Damon is on call for emergency decisions. And neither of them will have my phone number."

I look up, realizing I'm getting too attached to Helga's rear-end. "God, Jessie! I'm so impressed."

Jessie crosses her legs and beats a tattoo on her kneecap.

"I wasn't exactly thrilled by Dad's...requirements. But I'm trying to look at it this way: in the short time I've been in the biz, I've met a lot of people who are profoundly jaded. Some of them don't even like sex anymore. I'm thinking a virginal summer might be just the thing to recharge the batteries."

From somewhere in the building, I hear a woman screaming, repeatedly. Jessie hears it too, and cracks up.

"Whoops! Sorry, I should have warned you. I'm not doing any productions till the autumn, but meanwhile I'm renting the space to Damon. Wanna watch?"

"Wouldn't we be...intruding?"

She pulls a remote from her desk and fires up a monitor in the corner. A big-breasted redhead is perched on a bed, receiving doggie-style ministrations from a large black man.

"Horace!" says Jessie, clapping her hands together. "And Amber Day Lishus. What a pro."

Amber pounds back into Horace, letting out a series of yelps that gathers into a full-throated scream.

"Do you know that's not even fake? Amber says she's always screamed like that. Lost a couple boyfriends that way. And take note of the cheek-wobble! Just enough fat to produce that playful Jell-O jiggle. She is *such* a piece!"

I am compelled to agree. Horace pulls out and deposits a load of semen on Amber's cheeks. Amber makes a show of spreading it around, Horace produces an appreciative grin—then Damon decides they've got enough.

"Outstanding, Horace! Great fucking, Miss Amber. Let's all take a ten."

A crewmember passes towels to Amber and Horace, someone comes in to change the bedclothes, and the camera guys head outside for a smoke.

"Why don't I walk you out?" says Jessie. "I'm on the next shoot."

"Oh." I get up and follow her into the parking lot. "Are you…participating?"

"Nope. Just helping out. Picking up some tips from Damon. Maybe some fluff-work, if I'm feeling frisky.

"Fluff-work?"

"Hopkins! You don't know 'fluff-work'?"

"Um…no?"

"Keeping the guy erect between scenes. A little handwork, a little oral. Whatever it takes."

"Whatever it takes." I laugh and swing an arm around my wife's shoulder. I'm also taking classes," she says.

"Really?"

"Yeah. Psychology. Maybe a master's in sex therapy."

"Jessie! That's great."

We arrive at my car, and Jessie gets all shy, which seems tremendously out of place.

"I want you to visit this summer," she says, half to the ground. "Whenever you want. Call ahead and I'll make you dinner."

"Thanks, Jess. I will. You know…it's so good to see you happy."

"I finally got the formula, Hopkins. I'm a freak. And I *like* being a freak. And you've got Pisarro."

"Well, I…"

She puts a hand on my shoulder and presses with her fingers.

"It's love, Hop. Don't discount it. I hope to find it myself one day. You be good to her."

I've had enough miraculous statements for one night. "I'd…better get rollin'."

"Me, too," she says. "Give my love to those amazing children."

She places a hand on my jawline and gives me a courtly kiss.

"We did okay, Hopkins."

Damon pops out of the studio.

"Hey, Jess! Ready to roll?"

I head south on I-5 till the red sign drops from the rear-view. It occurs to me that I have done everything absolutely, profoundly wrong for the past fifteen years, and have been rewarded with the perfect life. There's your karmic balance. There's your just reward. The scientist pops up one more time to have a good laugh. Followed by my cell phone.

"Yello."

"Hi Dad. Can I go to bed now?"

"Yeah, son. I'll be back in an hour. Thanks for covering."

"No prob, dude."

It strikes me that Marcus has dropped the old-fashioned sayings. He's become a teenager, and may never say "Hell's bells" again.

"Oh, and Marcus?"

"Ye-es?"

"Your mother loves you."

"You mean Jessie?"

"I mean your mother."

Marcus laughs. "Just kidding, Dad. Good night."

"'Night, Marcus."

978-0-595-41807-7
0-595-41807-4

CPSIA information can be obtained at www.ICGtesting.com
Printed in the USA
BVOW08s2039100815

412668BV00001B/93/P